RIGHTEOUS KILL

A NOVEL

G. MICHAEL HOPF

DEDICATION

TO RICKY

"There are only two kinds of men: the righteous who think they are sinners and the sinners who think they are righteous."

Blaise Pascal

PROLOGUE

APRIL 17, 1885

OUTSKIRTS OF WALLACE, IDAHO TERRITORY

Each swing of the pickaxe reverberated through sixteen-year-old Billy Connolly's already sore body. He removed his tattered hat, wiped his sweaty brow with his sleeve, and grimaced at the rock he had just spent the last thirty minutes trying to pulverize. If he described his job as miserable, it would be an understatement. Billy despised what he did and never expected he'd have to work in a silver mine, yet here he was, the oldest son of an Irish immigrant. No, none of this was the plan his now deceased father had had for the Connolly family when they'd left Galway three years before, but then again, William Connolly Sr. wasn't supposed to die either.

After Billy's father died, Billy did what any responsible eldest son would do, and that was take work to support the family. With his mother and two younger siblings to care for, he took a job at one of the mines close by. It was hard physical labor, but until something else came around, Billy would have to keep swinging his pickaxe.

The workday ended like usual with the second shift

coming on and Billy taking his leave. His mind wandered to what life would have been if his father hadn't died upon their arrival in Wallace. He mostly was upset by the fact that he couldn't leave now. The dream of America was intoxicating, and he wanted so much to see the expansive landscape and devour all that his adopted land could give him. Feeling stuck by circumstance, he started to feel resentful and longed for the day he could be free, but when would that be, and what would he do?

As he came around the bend in the trail, his cabin came into sight. It wasn't much, a single-room log building with a tiny loft. It was too small for them even without his father. He took notice of two horses hitched out front and wondered who they could belong to.

Billy rode up alongside the horses and dismounted. He admired the beautiful saddlebags on the horse closest to him; the bag was embroidered with the initials DSG. He hitched his old mare and made his way to the front door, but before he reached it, the door swung open and out came two men; both were laughing.

The first man, who was tall and lean, his face covered with a thick beard, gave Billy a wink and said, "You have a nice mama."

Unsure what that meant, Billy asked, "What?"

The second man looked similar to the first, but stood a couple of inches shorter with a wider build. He walked up to Billy and stood inches from his face. He leaned in and sniffed. "Boy, you smell. I suggest you go take a bath."

Billy furrowed his brow and asked, "Who are you?"

It was then that he noticed the second man was buttoning the fly of his trousers.

"Just friends of your ma," the second man said.

Billy stood frozen to the spot, unsure what to do. His senses told him something was wrong, but he couldn't quite peg it. He glanced inside the cabin, but it was too dark to see anything.

The men unhitched their horses and mounted them.

Fear began to rise in Billy. He entered the darkened cabin and looked around. It took a second for his eyes to adjust, and when they did, he saw his mother in the corner crying, her dress torn. "Ma, what's going on?"

She pulled the torn top of her dress together to cover her bosom and replied, "It's nothing, William."

Dolores Connelly was a proud woman and not one prone to hysterics, so seeing her this way sent signals to Billy that something horrible had occurred. He marched over to her and asked, "What did those men do?"

Wiping tears from her reddened cheeks, she answered, "Just give me a moment. How about you go out and get cleaned up."

Billy's suspicions rose as to what had transpired, but it seemed all too surreal. *How could this happen?* he thought.

"Those men hurt Mama," Shannon, Billy's ten-year-old sister, said from the loft.

Billy shot her a look and asked, "Those men hurt Mama?"

"They came in and hit her. Then they threw her on the table, one man got on top, and—"

"Enough," Billy said, his anger rising.

"Shannon, you be quiet," Dolores said.

Stepping up inches from her, Billy asked, "Those men hurt you, didn't they?"

"It was my fault. I let them in; I shouldn't have. I'm a damn fool," she replied.

Billy's anger kept rising. He was exhausted from a job he hated, had recently lost his father, and now it appeared his mother had just been raped. He marched over to his mother's cot in the far corner, pulled aside the blanket that hung as a divider, and began searching under it.

"What are you doing?" Dolores asked.

His fingers touched the wooden box he was searching for, and he pulled it out. He set it on the mattress and opened it to find a Colt New Army pistol, with loose rounds lying in the bottom. He removed the pistol, examined it carefully, and confirmed it was loaded.

"William Connolly, what are you doing with that gun?" Dolores asked, her eyes wide with fear.

Billy jumped to his feet and shoved the pistol in his waistband. "Ma, I'm going to go kill those men."

She ran to the door and blocked it. "You won't do anything, you hear me?"

He got inches from her face and said, "Ma, I love you, but I can't live with this injustice."

"I can. Now put that back and go get cleaned up for dinner," she said, her body trembling.

From the loft Shannon and Michael, the youngest at eight years old, stared down on the scene in disbelief.

"No, I need to do this; otherwise they're liable to

4

come back again. Those men need to be taught a lesson."

"And if they come back, I'll handle it. I can't risk you getting hurt. I need you; your sister and brother need you," she snapped, her already swollen eyes tearing up.

"Pa wouldn't stand for this. I won't either," Billy declared.

"Your pa is dead; it doesn't matter what he'd do or not do. Now put that damn thing away and go get ready for dinner," she blared.

He stared into her tear-filled eyes. The last thing he wanted to do was forcibly move her, so he stepped back, turned and went to the cot. Using his body to cover his actions, he pretended to put the pistol away; instead he shoved it into the inside pocket of his trousers. He slid the box back under the cot and rose.

"Now go get yourself cleaned up. I'll have dinner on the table shortly," she said, sighing. She moved away from the door and walked over to the fireplace. There, she began to stir the contents of a cauldron that hung over the hot coals.

He stepped to the door and looked at her. His anger was at a tipping point, but he hid it. Deliberately slowing his tempo and keeping his voice low, he said, "I'm sorry, Ma."

Not looking at him, she kept stirring the stew, her sobs audible. Using her free hand, she wiped her tears and said, "Go get cleaned up, and take your siblings with you."

"You two, with me," Billy said.

Shannon and Michael climbed down the ladder and

walked over to Billy. He opened the door and said, "Out with ya. Go get cleaned up." The two raced out. Before stepping out himself, he said, "Get yourself cleaned up too, Ma."

Her voice cracking, she replied, "I will. Now go, give me a moment."

He exited the cabin and closed the door.

Shannon and Michael stood, their eyes fixed on him. "Whatcha going to do, Billy?" Shannon asked.

"I'm going to go get those men. I need you two to do as Ma said, get cleaned up, go back inside, and tell her I'm down at the shed putting the horse away."

"She's going to be mad," Shannon said while Michael nodded.

Billy could see by the look on Michael's face that he was traumatized by the attack. He cradled his head in his hand and said, "It'll be okay. Just do as your sister says."

"I'm scared," Michael said.

"I know you are, but I'm going to handle this," Billy said.

"But Ma told you not to," Michael reminded him.

"Sometimes us men have to do things that we're told not to do. You'll understand when you get older," Billy said, reciting something his father often told him. "Pa wouldn't have stood by and let this go unanswered; I can't either."

"But—" Michael said before being interrupted by Billy.

"Go get cleaned up now," Billy said. He strutted over to his horse and unhitched it. "I'll be back soon," he said as he mounted the horse and pulled the reins hard to the left.

Shannon and Michael watched as he rode off.

WALLACE, IDAHO TERRITORY

At every turn or bend in the road, Billy expected to run into the men. His heart would race with each anticipated encounter when he rounded a corner and found it empty. Onward like this his ride went until he reached town. He didn't know where they were or if they'd even gone to Wallace, but something told him they were there. Unsure where they would specifically be, he did have one thing to look for, and that was the black horse with the ornate saddlebags with the initials DSG.

He imagined men like that would be at a saloon, and with only two in town, he didn't have too many places to go. He rode up to the first saloon, Gavin's, and along the front side of it stood a row of hitched horses. He closely examined each one and didn't see the horse he was looking for, so he proceeded to the second and last saloon, The Panhandler. He slowly trotted by the horses out front, and after passing four, he came upon a large black horse. He stopped and saw the saddlebags. A surge of tension shot through him as he contemplated turning around, but he quickly brushed it off. He dismounted, hitched his horse, and stepped onto the walkway. In front of him were the swinging doors of the saloon; the raucous sound of merriment and laughter hit his ears. Before walking in, he pulled out the pistol and double-checked it was loaded.

The doors swung open, and in front of him was a man who was clearly intoxicated. He looked at Billy, then to his pistol, and joked, "Don't shoot." He stumbled off the walkway and into the street, singing a tune.

Billy shoved the pistol back into his belt. He took a deep breath and exhaled heavily. He knew the next step could change his life, but he was prepared for the consequences. He knew his father was looking down on him, and could not in good conscience just let this crime go unpunished. Summoning all his courage, he pushed the doors open and entered the saloon.

A few heads turned and looked, but he was quickly dismissed.

Billy scanned the room but didn't see the men. He cautiously walked towards the bar, his eyes darting from face to face, hoping to find them, but still he came up short. He reached the bar, turned and looked down to the left but didn't see them. He then craned his head right and looked, but again they weren't there.

"What will you have?" the bartender, a man named Charlie, asked.

"Oh, um, nothing," Billy replied nervously.

"Then what in the hell you doing in here, boy?"

"I, um...I'm looking for two men. One rides a black horse and he has a saddlebag with the initials DSG embossed on it."

Charlie raised his brow and, with his head cocked ever so slightly to the side, said, "You're looking for Daryl Gundry, and the other man would be his brother, Mitch."

Wanting to sound and look confident, Billy lengthened his spine and said, "That's them. Where can I find them?"

"Who's looking?" Charlie asked. "I don't recognize you."

"A friend," Billy said, regretting uttering the word the second he said it.

"Friend? You sure you're not his kid?"

"Where can I find them?" Billy asked again.

Charlie furrowed his brow and stared without saying a word.

Feeling the awkward tension, Billy asked, "Are they here?"

"Yeah, they're over there playing cards in the corner," Charlie said and pointed.

Billy snapped his head in the direction and looked, but still didn't see them. "Where?"

"The table in the corner," Charlie said. "Now piss off."

Billy stepped away from the bar and headed towards the corner. Each step he took proved more difficult than the last. His stomach churned and tightened as a state of fear gripped him, yet he kept moving forward until he was a foot from the table.

Five men sat around the small round table. The three he could see were not Daryl or Mitch, leaving the men whose backs were facing him to be his targets.

One of the men playing at the table glanced up from his cards and said to Billy, "No gawking. Move on."

The sounds of the room grew silent, and all Billy

could hear and feel was the thumping of his heart.

"Are you deaf, boy?" the man asked.

"I'm looking for Mitch and Daryl," Billy said.

Both of the men whose backs faced Billy turned their heads and looked over their shoulders.

"Who are you?" Mitch asked. He had been the first man Billy encountered leaving his cabin, leaving Daryl to be the other.

Billy remained quiet, his right arm hanging to his side. He could feel his hands shaking and sweat forming on his brow.

Daryl squinted and said, "You're the boy we saw when we left the cabin."

"Oh yeah." Mitch snickered.

Daryl burst into laughter, his blackened teeth showing as he cackled.

What fear Billy had melted away and was replaced with pure rage. He pulled the Colt from his belt, raised it, and hollered, "You raped my ma!"

The men at the table became instantly silent, with Mitch and Daryl giving Billy a hard stare.

"Put the gun down, boy," Mitch barked.

The silence spread around the saloon, with even the piano player stopping to see what was happening.

"Son, if you mean to gun us down, it would help if you cocked the hammer back first," Daryl sneered.

Billy's focus turned to the hammer. He raised his thumb to cock it back but was shoved back as Daryl shot to his feet and drew.

Daryl swung his pistol around, his thumb cocking

the hammer back on his pistol.

As if the world had slowed down, Billy watched the muzzle of Daryl's pistol come towards him.

Mitch now jumped up and went for his pistol.

Billy managed to get the hammer back before Daryl could bring his pistol around. Not hesitating a second, Billy pulled the trigger. The .45-caliber round shot from the barrel and struck Daryl squarely in the chest.

The force of the impact sent Daryl reeling back and into Mitch, causing him to fumble and drop his pistol. Both men went crashing to the ground, with Daryl, now dead, lying on top of Mitch.

The other players at the table jumped out of the way, giving space for Billy to advance.

Taking the advantage, Billy cocked the pistol again, took a step forward, and said to Mitch, "You raped my ma; now pay the price." He aimed at Mitch's head and fired.

With both men now dead, Billy stood in disbelief at what he'd just done.

"Damn, boy, you killed the Gundry brothers," a man said, his back plastered against the wall.

Billy looked up and said, "I don't know who they were, just that they raped my ma."

"Oh no," a voice said loudly.

Billy heard the clicking of a hammer going back followed by a stern voice. "Drop the pistol, son."

Out of the corner of Billy's eyes, he saw a towering man with a glimmering badge on his chest. "Sir, those men raped my ma."

"That may be, son, but I need you to drop the pistol and come with me," the man said. He was the local sheriff and went simply by the name Sheriff Mac, which was short for McDonough.

"Please believe me, sir," Billy said, his arm still outstretched with the pistol.

"Son, I ain't gonna ask again," Mac barked.

Billy dropped the pistol, raised both hands, and turned to face Mac.

Mac gave Billy the once-over and saw a scared boy. "Come along."

Billy walked past Mac and out of the saloon.

***

Back and forth, Billy paced the small iron cell, nervous that he'd be hanged for murdering the men, something he hadn't thought much about when he'd decided to go out and shoot them.

Mac sat in his chair, his legs up, reading a newspaper, a pipe clenched between his teeth.

"What's going to happen, Sheriff?" Billy asked, his voice cracking with fear.

"Well, son, typically you hang for murdering people," Mac replied nonchalantly.

Grasping the bars, Billy exclaimed, "But they raped my ma."

"You keep saying that, but until I hear your ma say it, it's just your word. You see, son, we need witnesses, not just the ramblings of a kid," Mac said, looking up from his paper. "Anyways, Deputy Evans went to go bring your ma here. Soon we'll find out."

"She'll tell you, you just wait, and, Sheriff, I'm not a kid. I'm sixteen, will be seventeen soon," Billy shot back.

The door to the office opened and in came a man wearing a marshal's badge. His name was Eric Hemsworth, and he was a Deputy United States Marshal.

"What can I do for you, Marshal?" Mac asked, putting his feet on the floor.

"I heard two men I'm after have been killed," Hemsworth said. He removed his wide-brimmed hat and smoothed his jet-black hair.

"Well, Marshal, we had two men killed just about an hour ago in The Panhandler Saloon," Mac said. "It's quite a coincidence you heard about that all the way in Coeur d'Alene."

Taking a seat in a chair in front of the sheriff's desk, Hemsworth leaned back and replied, "I just happened to be in town 'cause I heard the Gundry brothers were seen around these parts. I went into that saloon you just mentioned and heard about the shooting, and now I'm here."

"Word is the men killed were Daryl and…"

"And Mitch Gundry, right?" Hemsworth said.

"Correct," Mac said.

Hemsworth reached into his overcoat and pulled out a piece of paper. He unfolded it and set it in front of Mac on his desk. "Both men were wanted for murder, armed robbery and rape. Like I said, I've been on their trail for weeks. They're notorious and have killed two bounty hunters already."

Looking over the wanted poster, Mac smiled and said, "Is that so?"

"Yep, they've proven to be quite difficult to track down," Hemsworth said.

The entire time the sheriff and marshal were talking, Billy stood glued to their conversation, his hands white-knuckling the bars.

"Whoever killed those men must be a tough son of a bitch," Hemsworth said.

Mac's grin widened as he glanced over at Billy.

Catching the look, Hemsworth craned his head in Billy's direction. "You?"

"Yes, sir," Billy said. "They raped my ma, so I went and shot them."

"I'm waiting to hear from his ma if that's the case," Mac said.

"I can assure you, Sheriff, these men are capable, so I would say the boy's claim is most likely credible," Hemsworth said.

"I told you, Sheriff," Billy declared.

"But if you're holding him for a crime, he hasn't committed one in the eyes of the federal government. In fact, you should put a medal on him," Hemsworth said. "Those men were wanted in Idaho and Montana Territories."

"Well, Marshal, we follow due process here," Mac said defensively.

"Sheriff, those men were wanted dead or alive," Hemsworth clarified. "I think you should let the boy go."

Mac clenched his teeth and pondered for a moment, then shot up from his desk, grabbed the keys, and walked over to the cell. He unlocked the door and opened it wide. "You're free to go."

"Thank you, Sheriff," Billy said.

Hemsworth got up, walked over, and extended his hand. "Marshal Hemsworth. Nice to make your acquaintance."

Billy shook Hemsworth's hand and said, "Billy Connolly."

"Billy, have you ever killed a man before?"

"No, sir."

"Well, by the looks of it, you're damn good at it," Hemsworth said.

"I was just doing what I felt was right. I don't allow quarter for no one who hurts innocent women or children, no, sir. My pa always taught me to stand up for what's right and defend the weak."

"Your pa was a smart and wise man," Hemsworth said. "Ever consider working for the marshal's service?"

"No, sir, never thought of it. To be honest, I've never heard of it until now."

Picking up on an accent, Hemsworth asked, "Where are you from?"

"Ireland, sir."

"I'll tell you what, Bill Connolly, when you become a United States citizen, you look me up. I'll see about helping you out."

"Thank you, sir," Billy said. "I'm working in the mines now. I hate it. I'd so love to become a marshal."

"Just remember, you need to get naturalized first, understand?"

"Yes, sir," Billy said, nodding happily. Facing Mac, Billy asked, "Can I go now, Sheriff?"

"You're free, go," Mac said, motioning with his arms for him to move out the door.

"Oh, Sheriff, can I get my pistol back?" Billy asked.

Mac nodded. He walked to a table. On it sat a chest; he unlocked it and removed the pistol in question. He handed it to Billy and said, "No more killing people in town, if you don't mind."

"Unless they're wanted," Hemsworth quipped. "Wait, I almost forgot; you're due a bounty."

"What's that?" Billy asked.

"Those men you killed were wanted and had a bounty on their heads, meaning there was a cash reward for killing them or bringing them in," Hemsworth explained.

Billy's eyes widened. "Cash reward? How much?"

"Five hundred for both. If you're going to collect, you need to come to the US Marshal's office in Coeur d'Alene to collect," Hemsworth said.

"How far is that?" Billy asked.

"About a three days' ride west," Hemsworth replied. "You have a few months to collect; there's no rush."

Nodding, Billy said, "Thank you, Marshal, and you too, Sheriff."

"If you see my deputy, tell him I said there was no need to talk with your ma," Mac said.

"Okay," Billy said. He rushed from the office and

into the faint light of dusk. He couldn't believe his luck. He'd gone from a terrified but determined boy bent on retribution for his mother, to a bounty hunter who had just secured his first bounty against two hardened outlaws. He stepped off the walkway and into the street, stopping when he heard a voice call out.

"William Connolly," Dolores yelped.

Billy stared in the direction of his mother's voice and saw a wagon coming his way. He waited for its arrival, to find Deputy Evans, his mother, sister and brother on board.

Hearing the interaction from inside, Mac came out and said, "Deputy, the young lad is free to go."

Pulling the brake on the wagon, Evans said, "Very well, should I just ride them all back to their cabin?"

Dolores jumped from the wagon and embraced Billy. She gave him a tight hug, then pulled back and slapped him across the face. "That was for disobeying me." She looked over to Mac and said, "My son was only defending my honor."

"It's fine, ma'am, we believe him," Mac said.

"He's not in trouble?" Dolores asked.

"No, ma'am, he's not," Mac replied.

Hemsworth emerged from the office and asked, "Are you his mother?"

"I am," Dolores replied. "And who are you?"

"Deputy US Marshal Hemsworth, ma'am, and I should say that your son is a brave man. A hero, he killed two notorious outlaws," Hemsworth said.

Dolores gave Billy an odd look and asked, "Hero?"

"Ma, I made five hundred dollars for the family too," Billy declared.

"What's this?" Dolores asked, surprised by the announcement.

"It's true, Mrs. Connolly. He just needs to go to Coeur d'Alene to collect," Hemsworth agreed.

"If this matter is over, can I take my family back home?" Dolores asked.

"Yes, you can," Mac answered.

Billy helped his mother back into the wagon then jumped into the open back. As Evans turned the wagon around and headed in the direction of their cabin, Hemsworth cried out, "Don't forget to collect your bounty, and remember to look me up."

"Look him up? What does that mean?" Dolores asked Billy.

"It means I'm going to be a United States Marshal one day, Ma, that's what it means," Billy replied with a broad smile stretched across his face.

CHAPTER ONE

JULY 7, 1895

OUTSKIRTS OF MISSOULA, MONTANA

A strong wind whipped in from the northwest, portending the coming storm Billy knew was on the way. Even the smell of the air told him rain was coming, and this time of year also could bring lightning. What he prayed didn't occur was a forest fire from a strike if a thunderstorm rolled in. Since he'd become a Deputy US Marshal with the help of Marshal Hemsworth seven years before, he'd been witness to two fires, with one so large it destroyed a mining town east of Stumptown in northwestern Montana.

Outside of the fear of a fire, Billy welcomed the storm because it would provide him the cover he'd need. He and Hemsworth had been staking out a remote cabin outside Bozeman with the hopes of arresting an outlaw by the name of Two-faced Bob. Bob was wanted in four states, including Montana, for murder and fraud. He had run a gambling operation in South Dakota, which had been legal until he ran into financial issues, and that was where everything went downhill for Bob. He had defrauded some investors whom he'd promised would be partners in a new gambling hall and saloon, but when his scheme was found out to be fraudulent, he'd murdered the investors and fled the state. He had been sighted in a saloon in Bozeman after he'd tried to acquire a gambling hall, but managed to flee before being arrested by local police.

Hemsworth received word about Bob after he killed a marshal during a search of the Bozeman area. He and Billy had departed Idaho three weeks before and had managed to track Bob down to this remote cabin after much investigating and hunting.

Bob was a dangerous man, that was not in doubt, but he didn't seem to be a highly skilled killer, as he'd killed all of his victims by shooting them in the back. However, Billy and Hemsworth were not going to take any chances. Their plan was to allow the cover of night and the storm to hide their movements up to the cabin; then they'd burst through the door and arrest Bob in his sleep. As far as plans go, it was simple and clear cut, but after having worked the job for seven years now, Billy knew all plans never seemed to go as they should.

As they waited for the sun to set, Hemsworth and Billy took up a watch position high in a rock outcropping that overlooked the cabin, which sat nestled in a gorge between three steep hillsides. The only way in and out was a narrow trail to the south, where they had a commanding view as well as a vantage point on the hillsides surrounding. If Bob were to leave now, they'd be able to nab him, and if he tried to flee up one of the hillsides, he'd be hard-pressed if under fire.

Billy felt confident in this arrest, as did Hemsworth,

and wanted to do just that, arrest him alive. Of course they could kill him, but after having murdered a fellow marshal, they wanted Bob to suffer as long as possible and eventually swing from a noose until dead.

"I haven't asked, how's your mother?" Hemsworth asked as he rolled a cigarette.

"I received a letter from her just before we came to Montana. She's doing well, but I know things must be tough for her since Michael left. I've offered for her to come to Coeur d'Alene and live in my house, so I'll see what she says."

"You're a good son," Hemsworth teased.

"Are you mocking me?"

"You could say that."

"I miss my ma, and I feel bad that my sister up and left her for that son of a bitch barkeep. I still to this day don't know what got into her. She should be taking care of Ma, but she'd rather run a damn bar with her drunkard of a husband."

"I'll offer one more time. If you want him to disappear, I know people who can help with that," Hemsworth offered sincerely.

"We're lawmen; we don't do those sorts of things."

"Look at it this way, we'd be saving your sister's life and quite possibly any offspring they might have."

"Don't get me wrong, I've thought about it, but it's her life. I just don't know what got into Shannon. She was always a good girl growing up," Billy said.

"People change."

"They do or they don't. What if she was always

harboring those types of sentiments?"

"At least she's not breaking the law, she's just living beneath her abilities is all," Hemsworth said.

Billy thought about his comment and said, "That's my greatest disappointment. I know she has potential and she's squandering it."

"Well, my friend, we can't control others, no matter how much we want to."

"I saw you received a letter in Missoula. Was it from Belinda?" Billy asked, referring to Hemsworth's wife.

"It was. She thinks she might be pregnant."

Billy's eyes widened with surprise. "Pregnant? Congratulations. Why didn't you tell me before?"

"Didn't have time," Hemsworth lied.

"Time? It took us three hours to ride out here; you could have mentioned it then," Billy said, chastising him.

Hemsworth's face shifted down.

Even in the dim light, Billy noticed his dour look. "What's wrong?"

"I didn't tell you because this is the third time in two years she's been pregnant. She's had a miscarriage the other two times," Hemsworth confessed.

"I'm sorry for your loss. I didn't know."

"Of course you wouldn't know. We never told anyone except our parents."

"If you don't want to talk about it, I understand," Billy said.

"Good, 'cause I don't, and please don't mention anything to anyone, especially don't tell Belinda when you see her next. She'll have me drawn and quartered if she knew I told you."

"Your secret will die with me."

The door of the cabin creaked open.

Billy swiftly spun around, picked up a set of binoculars, and peered down at the cabin. "Where do you suppose he's going?"

"Probably to relieve himself," Hemsworth replied. He was also spying on Bob through his own set of binoculars.

"And you're right," Billy said, lowering the binoculars. He turned back around and sighed. "This day is lasting forever."

Still watching Bob, Hemsworth said, "He's done and back inside the cabin."

"I wish we could just shoot him and be done with this," Billy complained.

Sitting back down in his spot, Hemsworth said, "He doesn't deserve an easy kill; he needs to suffer."

"I suppose we could make him suffer."

"We could, but that wouldn't be right."

"How well did you know Abbott?" Billy asked, referring to the marshal Bob had murdered.

"Well enough, he was a good man, one of the honest ones."

"Not all of us are, and it's disappointing," Billy said. He was referencing the fact that not all the marshals in service had integrity or operated within the laws they were sworn to enforce. The power of being a United States Marshal had gone to some people's heads, and they often abused it. "I still can't believe the story about that marshal in Arizona. It was shocking to hear that he was essentially a paid killer."

"That one gave us all a black eye," Hemsworth said. "Promise me, kid, that you'll stay honest and true."

"Of course, I wouldn't do this job otherwise."

"I know it can be easier to cut corners or skirt the law while saying you're enforcing it, but we have to stand above everyone else. We have to have standards, ethics."

Billy nodded because he was a believer in everything Hemsworth said.

Giving Billy a look, Hemsworth asked, "Promise me."

"Oh, you weren't saying that rhetorically?"

"No, I wasn't," Hemsworth insisted.

"I promise, as God is my witness, I'll never stray from the law or take matters into my own hands," Billy declared.

"Good man," Hemsworth said. "I knew you were an upright fellow the second I met you back in Wallace those many years ago. I understood what you did and why you did it."

"But what I did could be considered skirting the law."

"I suppose I should rephrase it and say we should always do what's morally right."

"Even if it's against the law?" Billy asked. He enjoyed the philosophical conversations and debates he often had with Hemsworth.

"You see, that's where the rub is. We're here to enforce the law and bring those outlaws to justice. When you were a kid, you technically could have been tried, but your sheriff used his discretion and let you go because of who you killed and why. I suppose it pertains to the circumstances."

"What if we go down, kick Bob's door down, tie him up, then torture him for a bit, then drag him behind our horses until we get to Bozeman?"

"Torture? I don't think I could do that, no matter how upset I am about what Two-faced did to one of our own," Hemsworth said.

"Well, I think a bit differently. Sometimes I think we need to act more like the people we hunt in order to fight them effectively."

"That's an interesting take. I've never heard you express that before," Hemsworth said.

"It's merely a thought exercise, nothing more," Billy confessed.

"You know what I like about you?"

"My bright smile and jovial demeanor?" Billy quipped.

"No, although those run a close second. I like that you think, but you don't overthink so much you can't do your job correctly."

"I'll take that as a compliment," Billy said, his chest puffed out.

"It is a compliment," Hemsworth said. "Say, how about you get an hour or so of shut-eye? I'll keep an eye out for ole Bob."

"Don't you go and take all the glory now. Wake me if he stirs," Billy said, scooting down enough to stretch out along the hard rocky ground.

"I would never do that," Hemsworth joked.

Billy covered his face with his hat and closed his eyes. Within a couple of minutes he was asleep.

***

"Wake up," Hemsworth said as he pushed Billy to get him awake.

Billy rose quickly, his hat falling onto the ground. "What is it?" he asked, looking around but unable to see due to the dark of night.

"It's time."

"What time is it?" Billy asked as he got his bearings in the darkness. He'd been fast asleep for three hours.

"I don't know, but it's been a good two hours since the sun set. I've been watching the cabin, and his lantern just dimmed about twenty minutes ago. That's a good sign."

Billy hopped to his feet, fumbled around for his rifle, and got ready for the assault.

The two made their way down the rocky slope. Each footfall they took was deliberate, ensuring they didn't slip and career down.

Reaching the bottom, Hemsworth whispered, "Let's do this as we planned. I go in first; you come in behind me."

"I didn't think about it being so damn dark," Billy complained as he tripped over a rock.

"Christ, Billy, don't fall down," Hemsworth mocked.

The men slipped up to the cabin without making a sound. Hemsworth took the right side of the door while Billy took the left.

Whispering, Hemsworth said, "On a count of three. One, two, three."

Billy stepped back and kicked the door in.

Hemsworth ran into the cabin, rifle at the ready, and up to a sleeping Bob in the cot. "US Marshals. You're under arrest!"

Bob's eyes sprang open. He shot up and went for his pistol on a table next to him, but before he could grab it, Billy came up and slammed the butt of his Winchester into the side of his head. Bob flopped on the floor unconscious.

"Let's get him loaded up. Time for him to receive the justice he deserves," Hemsworth said with a devilish smile.

CHAPTER TWO

JULY 8, 1895

TWO MILES SOUTH OF GREAT FALLS, MONTANA

Alice grunted as she pulled hard on the rock. She'd been working since before the sun had risen and was already feeling the fatigue weighing on her.

"Get out of there, you darn rock," she growled as she pulled hard.

"Why can't we just leave it?" Martha, Alice's nine-year-old sister, asked, her long brown hair blowing in the gentle breeze.

Alice cocked her head and glared at Martha. "If you worked as much as you ask questions, then we'd have this garden bed ready."

"But Ma said—" Martha said before being interrupted.

Alice gave a hard tug, and the chunk of granite pulled free. She held the rock, admiring it for a moment before tossing it on a pile of others. "I don't care what Ma said or says, period."

"You're not nice." Martha scowled.

Wiping her sweaty brow, Alice replied, "You're right, I'm not nice, but I'm the only thing you have right now."

"What about Grandma?"

"And her too, but the poor thing is getting too senile to even remember our names."

"When will Ma be well?" Martha asked, stooping down to pick up a smaller rock. She walked over and placed it on the growing pile.

Digging her hands through the loose dirt, Alice answered her sister's question bluntly. "When she puts down the bottle, that's when."

"She's just sad, that's all. Ever since Pa died, she's not been the same," Martha said.

"I know her excuse, and I'm sad that Pa died too, but in life we have responsibilities, and it's important that we live for the living. The dead are gone," Alice said sternly.

"But Ma's just sad. One day she'll stop being sad."

"That might be, but if we sit around and wait for that day, we might have died from starvation."

Martha teared up.

Hearing her crying, Alice stopped digging and gave Martha a sympathetic look. "Come here."

"You're mean," Martha barked.

"Please come here," Alice said, feeling regretful that she'd been harsh in her tone.

Martha reluctantly stepped over to Alice.

Wrapping her arms around Martha's small frame, Alice pulled her down and onto her lap. Whispering into her ear, she said, "I love you, sister, and I love Ma and Grandma. I get tired is all, and I do wish with all my heart that Ma will get better. I miss the old days. I miss Pa especially. I think that he really was the foundation this family stood upon, but you know what? He'd want us to keep moving forward; he'd want us to be strong."

"I miss him too," Martha wept.

"I'll promise you this. I'll try harder to be nicer to you and to Ma, okay?" Alice offered sincerely.

Martha nodded. The tears streamed down and turned the dirt on her face to streaks of mud.

"You girls hungry?" Grandma cried out from the porch of their two-story house.

"Is your tummy ready for breakfast?" Alice said as she tickled Martha's stomach.

Nodding, Martha said, "Yes."

"Good, let's go get cleaned up and have some eggs," Alice said.

The two got to their feet, but before they stepped off, Alice said, "I love you very much, and I want you to know that I'll do anything to keep you safe."

"What about Ma?"

"And Ma too, as well as Grandma," Alice replied.

Martha took Alice's hand and squeezed it.

A smile creased across Alice's face. She truly did love her family, including her mother, but the past four months since her father died had been hard on them all, with her mother turning to heavy drinking to numb her grief. As it pertained to Martha, she was a sweet and sensitive little girl who never had a harsh word for anyone and loved all things, including the animals they raised. Alice would often marvel at how two children from the same parents could be so different in personality, and could only explain that it was just God's hand.

"Get in here, girls. Breakfast is getting cold!" Grandma hollered.

"Coming, Grandma!" Alice called out as she and Martha marched across the field to the house.

MISSOULA, MONTANA

"Canada?" Hemsworth asked, his tone displaying his shock at the news he'd just been given.

"You heard right. I know this isn't what we wanted, but word has come down from the governor's office and was relayed from the Department of State via the Department of Justice back in Washington, DC," Phillip Smithers, the United States Attorney for the district, said.

"Who is he that it would warrant the attention from all the way back east?" Billy asked.

"Who knows, but the Canadians want him, and we've agreed to turn him over," Phillip said.

Hemsworth got up from his chair and paced the room. He stopped at a bookcase filled with leather hardbound law books. He was amazed by the total number. Curious, he asked, "Did you have to read all of these?"

Phillip furrowed his brow at the odd and untimely question, smiled and said, "No, we don't have to read each word."

"I heard you had to do a lot of reading and whatnot in order to get your job, but, lord, that would have been a bit much for me." Hemsworth laughed.

Putting his attention back on the topic, Phillip said,

"You two are instructed to escort Bob, or Alfred Cummins, as that is his real name, to Havre, about a day's ride south of the United States and Canadian border. You'll meet a Captain Jones with the North-West Mounted Police and turn him over. You'll escort them the rest of the way to the border and ensure they get across safely. They'll then take him to Vancouver, where he'll be tried for bribery, murder…anyway, there's a list of items here that Bob is wanted for up north."

Walking back to his chair, Hemsworth asked, "You don't know anything about who Bob—"

"Alfred," Billy quipped, interrupting Hemsworth.

"No, I don't know anything, but this wire hit my desk days ago. I knew if you captured him, you'd be a bit upset, as I am, but we have an arrangement with our cousins to the north, and we're handing him over, simple as that."

"But he murdered a United States Marshal," Hemsworth blared.

"I'm aware of what he's done, but we have our orders. Now I suggest you two get prepared for your journey," Phillip said.

Billy and Hemsworth got up, said their goodbyes, and left the office. In the lobby of the federal government building, Hemsworth couldn't hold in his contempt for what had just transpired. "I can't believe this."

"Have you ever heard of anything like this before?" Billy asked.

Hemsworth had been a marshal for fifteen years, so his knowledge was vast. "I have, but something is off about this."

"What can we do?" Billy asked.

Hemsworth stood, his mind spinning.

"Listen, old friend, let's go get cleaned up, then go have a nice dinner. We'll set out tomorrow afternoon. What do you say?" Billy asked.

The question tore Hemsworth from his thoughts. "Sure, that sounds good. Let's add having a few drinks as well. I need something to dull my senses tonight."

TWO MILES SOUTH OF GREAT FALLS, MONTANA

Four figures, all on horseback, emerged from the tree line and stopped at the road, the bright light of the full moon casting shadows on the ground.

"I'm hungry and don't think I can settle for what's in my saddlebag," Gus said as he eyed the house in the distance.

"We have our orders. Make no contact with anyone, just head straight for the cabin, and return," Harry replied.

"Harry, I'm with Gus, and Henry here agrees. Let's go find a house to get something else to eat, maybe even bunk down for the night," Joseph said as he pulled tighter on the reins of his horse to calm it down.

"No, we keep going another few miles and bed down in the woods somewhere out of sight," Harry snarled.

Gus, a large man, towering six feet four inches, scowled at Harry and said, "You're not our boss."

"You're right, I'm not, but we all have a common one, and he said we ride straight for the cabin, grab Al, and bring him back. We can't risk being seen or any other suspicion," Harry shot back.

Henry, who unlike Harry, was short in stature, reared his horse back and said, "I say we vote on it."

Gus nodded and said, "Good idea."

"I agree with Gus." Joseph snorted then spit on the ground. He wiped what saliva remained on his thick beard with his sleeve. "Plus, I'm filthy. I need to wash up, and I don't want to do so in a cold creek."

"All in favor of finding a hospitable host for the night say aye," Gus said.

"Damn it, fellas, we can't be doing this," Harry barked.

"Aye," Joseph said.

"Aye," Henry replied.

"Gus, damn it, this could be our undoing," Harry snapped.

"Aye," Gus said happily. "You lost, Harry, sorry, but we're going to find a nice hot meal and maybe even a bath and bed."

"That house over there looks like it could work. Let's give it a try," Joseph said, pointing to the two-story house just across the road and field beyond.

"This is a mistake, I'm telling you," Harry said.

Slapping Harry on the back, Gus said, "Ain't nothing going to happen, now come on."

Henry and Joseph nudged their horses forward, leaving Gus and Harry by themselves.

"Gus, we don't know who those folks are. We can't be riding in and making ourselves at home. How will we explain what we're doing here?" Harry asked.

"We'll lie, Harry; we've been doing that for a long time. Now c'mon, I can already taste a hot meal." Gus laughed. He rode off and caught up with Henry and Joseph.

Harry sat and watched as the others rode towards the house. A sense in him yelled out that nothing but trouble was about to happen, but outnumbered, he couldn't do a thing but go along with it in hopes that he could mitigate any issues that might arise.

***

Finding it hard to read due to the poor lighting, Alice turned up the flame on the lantern. With the large orange flame illuminating brighter, she went back to reading *Moby-Dick*, a book she'd been gifted for Christmas.

The sounds of horses' hooves came from outside.

She peered through the window, which overlooked the front drive, but she couldn't see anything. She dimmed the light and looked again, and this time saw four riders circling in the front yard.

Downstairs, she heard muffled chatter followed by her mother speaking loudly about hearing something outside.

Alice could tell by the tone and tenor of her mother's voice that she was intoxicated. She kept a close eye on the men outside as they dismounted their horses and hitched them up to the railing of the porch.

Downstairs, her mother, whose birth name was Margaret but went by Maggie, stumbled to the door, a shotgun in her hands.

"Don't go out there shooting. See who they are first," Anne, who was Alice's grandma, barked from her rocking chair in front of the fireplace. On her lap was a sweater she was knitting.

Maggie unlatched the door, flung it open, and stepped outside, the shotgun at hip level.

"Whoa there, lassie!" Gus laughed. "Put the gun down. We're not here to hurt anyone."

"Ma'am, we've ridden a long way and are tired and in need of a hot meal. I know what we're asking might seem rude, but could you spare a hot plate of something?" Harry asked, his tone gentle.

"Who are you?" Maggie said, her speech slurred.

The men glanced at each other. They could see by the way Maggie was talking and her weaving she was very drunk.

"Like my associate Harry said, ma'am, we're just tired; plus we haven't had a hot meal in about a week or so," Henry said.

"It would be real nice of you, and we'd be most appreciative, ma'am," Joseph said.

Out of an abundance of caution, all the men stayed atop their horses just in case Maggie decided to start shooting.

"Who are you? I won't ask again!" Maggie barked, this time raising the shotgun to her shoulder.

Raising his arms defensively, Harry said, "Ma'am, we mean no harm. We were just inquiring is all."

"You all get; there ain't nothing here for you!" Maggie spat.

"Maybe if we talked to the man of the house, we could explain," Gus said.

Maggie swung the muzzle of the shotgun towards Gus and hollered, "There ain't no man of the house here; now get!"

Anne appeared at the door. "You gentlemen had best get going. My daughter here has had a bit to drink, and she's known for having a heavy trigger finger."

Upstairs, filled with competing emotions, Alice watched the encounter.

Joseph caught sight of Alice and waved.

"Who are you waving to?" Maggie barked as she now pointed the barrel of the shotgun at Joseph.

"Just that pretty little face in the window up there," Joseph replied, again waving to Alice, who now ducked behind the curtain.

Maggie pointed the shotgun into the air and pulled the trigger, releasing one barrel of shot into the night sky. "Get!"

"Okay, ma'am, we got your point. We're headed out," Harry said. "C'mon, boys, we're not welcome here."

The men turned their horses around.

Alice peeked through the corner of the blind; her heart raced from the exhilaration of the tense encounter.

Maggie stood, her body subtly bobbing back and forth.

Unable to leave without taunting Maggie, Joseph waved to the window where he'd seen Alice and blew a kiss.

Seeing this filled Maggie with rage. She pointed the barrel at Joseph, put her index finger on the trigger, and began to apply pressure. But before she could fire, Anne stepped forward and lowered the muzzle until it was pointed at the ground. "Ease up, Maggie, ease up."

"Mom, these men are up to no good, I can tell," Maggie spat.

"That may be, but let's not go shooting them for no good reason," Anne said.

Harry tipped his hat and said, "Good evening, and please pardon us, we met no harm."

Maggie remained quiet. She glared at Harry with a look that told him she would really kill any of them if they came back.

Harry gave Maggie and Anne one last look, pulled the reins on his horse to the left, and trotted away, with the other men following just behind. When they were a distance away, Joseph pulled back on his horse and came to a full stop. He adjusted himself in the saddle and asked, "Boys, are you thinking what I'm thinking?"

Gus stopped and replied, "I think I am."

"No, we're moving on. Now let's go," Harry said.

Henry too had stopped and pulled up alongside Joseph. "I'm with you."

"Whatever you have planned, it's not going to happen. We're not even supposed to be here. Remember, we're being paid to secretly come in and get out," Harry said.

"Then no one will know," Gus snorted.

"I like how you think," Joseph said.

"No!" Harry barked.

"I've already said it, you're not in charge of us. If we want to go back, then we'll go back," Gus snapped back to Harry.

"You boys are fools. We're not here to get into trouble; we're here to do our job, nothing more," Harry said.

"Where did they find you, the local church?" Joseph laughed.

Gus and Henry weren't notorious outlaws, but they definitely violated the law as often as they could, most of the times unintentionally, as they did whatever they wanted to do without thought of whether it was legal or not. However, Joseph was a wanted criminal and was known by the name Killer Joe; this was a secret he was keeping to himself. His rationale for being there was also different than the other three. He was there to make money, but it was Al's money he was after. It was rumored that Al had a large amount stashed away. Harry, on the other hand, was neither a criminal nor a man who lived on the edge. He was a God-fearing family man who merely needed honest work but had ended up with less than desirable men to work alongside.

"If you all are done with these fantasies, let's move on. We'll try the next house we come upon to see if they'll give us some hot food," Harry proposed, hoping his compromise would get them to follow him. He started to trot away and noticed none of the others were following him. He stopped and hollered back, "Come on, let's move."

"We're not going," Joseph said.

"Yes, you are," Harry said, turning back and trotting up to them.

"No, we're not," Joseph replied emphatically.

Harry shook his head in disgust and asked, "Is this who you are? You're really going to ride back and take advantage of those women?"

"Harry, if you go to an orchard and pick the low-hanging fruit from the tree, is that considered taking advantage of the tree?" Gus asked.

"Stop this insane talk and let's keep moving," Harry pleaded.

"You go ahead. We'll meet you at the next town in a few hours," Joseph said.

"I'm not letting you go back to that house and hurt those women," Harry said, pulling his pistol from its holster. He cocked it and said, "Now let's move on."

The other three looked at each other, with Gus speaking first. "He's right. This is stupid. Let's ride on until the next house."

"Don't back down," Joseph said.

"I think Harry might be right," Henry admitted. "Let's keep moving on to Missoula."

"Cowards," Joseph spat.

Gus and Henry moved alongside Harry, who still had his pistol out and now trained on Joseph.

"You're outnumbered now, Joe. Let's go," Harry

said, his full attention on Joseph.

Safely out of the way, Gus pulled his horse next to Harry's, pulled his pistol, cocked it and placed it against the back of Harry's head. "Drop it."

Stunned by the sudden turnaround, Harry did as Gus ordered and let go of his pistol.

"I don't much like being told what to do, not by you or anyone. We're just trying to have a good time, and all you care about is being a pain in everyone's ass."

"I just want us to do our job, that's all," Harry said.

"We're going to go back, but you, you're going to stay here," Gus said. "Henry, tie him up over there." Gus nodded towards a wooden split-rail fence.

"You don't have to do that," Harry begged.

"Yeah, we do," Gus said.

Henry dismounted his horse, took a line of rope from his saddlebag, and said, "Hop off, Harry."

Harry climbed down from his horse and followed Henry to the fence, where his arms were bound behind his back and tied to a fence rail. When Henry finished securing the last knot, he patted Harry on the shoulder and said, "You should get some shut-eye. We'll be gone for a bit."

"You're making a mistake," Harry said. "This could go terribly wrong."

"Best you stay quiet," Gus said, chuckling.

The three men rode back towards the house, their laughter filling the air.

MISSOULA, MONTANA

"Bartender, two more," Hemsworth said, his speech slurred.

The bartender walked up and set the entire bottle of whiskey down. "Just tell me when you've had your fill."

"Fair enough," Billy said, snatching the bottle and filling their glasses. He picked his up and said, "A toast."

Taking his glass in his hand, Hemsworth asked, "To what are we toasting now?"

"Our lives."

"Lives?"

"Maybe it's the booze talking, but I'm grateful that I can do what I do. If I had never met you, I wouldn't be here today. More than likely I would have been working a mine," Billy explained.

"Cheers to you not having to work in the mines," Hemsworth said, tapping Billy's glass.

"Yes, cheers to me not having to work in those silver mines," Billy said and tossed the whiskey back.

A woman approached the bar. She gave Billy an alluring gaze and took a spot next to him. "I haven't seen you in here before," she purred.

Billy leaned back, squinted and said, "On account I've never been here."

"What brings you to Missoula?" she asked.

"Well, I'm here because—"

Interrupting Billy, Hemsworth said, "Ma'am, you don't need to ask questions, just take my friend upstairs with you."

She touched Billy's arm and asked, "Do you want to go upstairs and get to know me better?"

Billy's face turned red. Unable to look at her, his eyes darted to the floor.

She leaned in and said, "My name is Beatrix, but everyone calls me Trixie."

"Trixie, hey?" Hemsworth asked, finding her allure attractive.

"So what do you say?" she asked Billy, while ignoring Hemsworth's comment.

"I'm fine. I'll just stay down here," Billy replied.

"Oh, come on, you're not married; go have some fun," Hemsworth said, nudging Billy with his elbow.

"No, I'm fine," Billy asserted, his tone more forceful than before.

"Oh, why not? You look like you could use some company," Trixie said, petting Billy's arm more aggressively.

"No," Billy said and stormed off.

"What's the matter with him?" she asked flippantly, a look of irritation on her face.

"I don't know," Hemsworth answered.

Giving Hemsworth a once-over, she asked, "How about you, then?"

"I'm married, happily, so best you go find someone else," Hemsworth replied. He grabbed the bottle of whiskey from the bar, tossed the bartender a few coins, and headed towards Billy, who was now leaning against the far wall near the stairwell.

The bar was a two-story building, with the doors to

the upstairs rooms overlooking the main bar area below.

"Something wrong?" Hemsworth asked.

"I don't like prostitutes," Billy snapped.

"All you had to do was say so. I didn't mean anything by it."

"Just don't do that again," Billy snapped.

"Noted," Hemsworth said. He filled Billy's glass, then his own, and continued, "What shall we toast to now?"

Looking dour, Billy replied, "To Bob getting the justice he deserves."

"That's a good one," Hemsworth said, touching his glass to Billy's. "Say, who do you think this Alfred character is?"

"I don't know, but you should send a wire to Coeur d'Alene and see if they can help shed some light on him," Billy proposed.

"That's not a bad idea. I think I'll do that once we're done here," Hemsworth said, pulling his pocket watch out to see what time it was.

Billy placed his glass on an empty table near him and said, "I'm finished anyway. Let's head to the Western Union and fire that telegram off. I want to find out more about Alfred sooner rather than later."

Putting the cork back in the bottle, Hemsworth said, "You were serious about knowing, weren't ya?"

"Dead serious," Billy said, wanting to just stay busy.

"Then let's go," Hemsworth said with a crooked smile on his face.

CHAPTER THREE

JULY 9, 1895

TWO MILES SOUTH OF GREAT FALLS, MONTANA

Gus, Henry and Joseph waited for the last light to go out before making their way down the drive. After seeing how Maggie was before, the last thing they wanted to do was barge in and be greeted with her double-barreled shotgun.

"I've got dibs on the girl in the window," Joseph grunted as he spit tobacco juice on the ground. A dribble of saliva clung to his thick beard. He wiped his chin and snickered. "She looks like she could use a hug."

"You're a sick bastard," Gus said.

"Don't pay no mind to what I do. You worry about yourself," Joseph said.

"You suppose they have any money socked away?" Henry asked.

"I suppose so. We'll search for it when we're finished having our fun," Gus replied.

The men quietly walked up to the front porch and stopped.

"Let's do this," Joseph said, stepping forward.

Gus grabbed his arm and stopped him. "No, we can't go kicking the door in. I suspect their bedrooms are upstairs. If we go in making a bunch of noise, it will alert the mother. I suspect she sleeps with that shotgun."

"Then how the hell are we going to get in?" Joseph growled.

"We check to see if any window or door is open," Gus replied.

"And what if none are?" Joseph asked.

"Then we go in like you want to," Gus said.

Joseph grunted. He shrugged off Gus' grasp and walked quietly up to the front door, gingerly placing each foot on the steps so they wouldn't creak under his weight. He reached the door, grasped the knob, and tried to turn it, only to find it locked. He looked over his shoulder and whispered, "Locked."

Henry was at the front window but, like the door, found it secured.

Meanwhile, Gus made his way around the side of the house. He found a window there, tried to open it, but it too was locked.

The creaking of the back door sounded.

Gus froze.

Footfalls could be heard heading away from the house.

Gus quietly made his way to the corner of the house and peered around. The full moon provided enough light to make out a small figure heading towards the outhouse. He turned the knob but found it locked.

Henry and Joseph made their way to Gus.

"I heard a noise," Joseph whispered.

"It's the child, I believe," Gus replied.

"Perfect," Joseph said. He stepped away from the other two but again was stopped by Gus.

"Just wait," Gus warned.

Shrugging off his grasp once more, Joseph spat, "I'm not waiting anymore. You know the damn door is unlocked; go do your thing and leave me be." He briskly headed to the outhouse.

"Damn fool. We'd best hurry up and get inside before he wakes everyone up," Gus said.

The two raced around the back, up the small set of stairs and into the house.

Joseph walked up to the door of the outhouse; a thrill shot through him. He knew he was a despicable man but didn't care. He knew he was slated for hell as it was, so why not just keep doing devious and disgusting things, he thought. He took the latch of the outhouse door in his hand, lifted it, and threw the door wide open. With a devilish grin stretched across his face, he said, "Hey there." His grin melted away when he saw it wasn't Alice. "Who are you?"

Martha sat staring in terror at Joseph.

Seeing she was about to scream, Joseph pulled a six-inch knife from a sheath on his belt and held it out. "You make one sound, I'll cut your throat."

Martha began to whimper.

"Be quiet," Joseph warned.

Martha's whimpering quickly turned to sobbing. Under her breath she pleaded, "Don't hurt me, please."

Joseph stepped closer to her, placed his left hand over her mouth, and put the blade to her throat. "Ssh."

Inside the house, Gus and Henry slowly navigated the darkened space until they reached the stairs.

Gus peered through the pitch black, his heart pounding.

Just behind him, Henry stood anxiously waiting for Gus to move.

Craning his head back, Gus whispered, "Be quiet and follow my lead."

"Okay," Henry replied.

Back outside, Joseph was stumped on what to do. He stood silent, staring at the trembling child. "I'm going to remove my hand. And when I do, I need you to tell me where I can find your sister. Do you understand?"

Martha nodded.

"And if you scream, I won't just slit your throat, I'll go inside and kill everyone. Do you understand?"

Martha again nodded.

"Good," Joseph said. He slowly removed his hand and asked, "Are you ready to get up and take me inside?"

With tears flowing down her face, Martha nodded.

Joseph stepped back and said, "Now come."

Martha reached for old newspaper so she could wipe but was stopped.

"Now," Joseph barked.

Fearing for her life, Martha did as he said and stood up without wiping herself.

Joseph grabbed her by the back of her head and pulled her out of the outhouse. Wrapping his fingers through her hair, he pulled her head towards his and said, "No screaming."

"I won't," she whimpered.

"Good, now take me to where your sister sleeps," Joseph said and pulled her towards the back door.

Gus and Henry were slowly scaling the stairs and heard the footfalls of Martha and Joseph at the back door. They paused a few steps shy of the landing and listened.

When Martha entered the house, all she could think about was her family. She knew if she didn't cry out, they would suffer at the hands of this stranger, and her death could follow. She didn't know him nor what he was capable of. But if she did warn her mother and the others, maybe she'd have a chance; at least they would. Quickly making up her mind, she pulled away from Joseph and yelled, "Mama, Alice, wake up, wake up!"

Hearing Martha cry out, Gus and Henry froze.

Alice heard the cry from her little sister and opened her eyes.

"Alice, Mama, wake up! There's a bad man in the house!" Martha bellowed as she sprinted through the kitchen.

"Damn you!" Joseph barked as he went in pursuit.

Martha dodged the table, but as she went to clear the doorway, her shoulder struck the doorjamb, spun her around, and caused her to fall to the floor hard.

Knowing the element of surprise was now gone, Gus and Henry cleared the remaining stairs and burst through the first door they came to. The lantern on her nightstand was lit just enough to cast a slight glow, allowing them to see Maggie going for the shotgun.

Gus ripped his pistol from his holster, cocked it, and took a shot at Maggie. The bullet smashed into the wall behind her.

Henry leapt across the bed, grabbed her arm, and pulled her to the ground. "I got her, I got her."

Gus ran up to help Henry, who was wrestling with Maggie on the floor.

"Get off me!" Maggie spat.

"Settle down and we won't hurt you or your family," Henry snapped.

Ignoring his warning, Maggie leaned her face towards his, opened her mouth wide, and bit down on Henry's cheek. She twisted and pulled her head away, forcibly tearing a chunk of flesh off.

Henry wailed in pain. He rolled off her and onto the floor, his hands covering the wound on his face.

Maggie didn't hesitate, she jumped to her feet, but before she could even make an attempt to grab the shotgun, Gus slammed the butt of the revolver into the back of her head.

The blow was enough to knock her out. She collapsed to the floor.

Downstairs, Joseph got to Martha and pulled her small body off the floor, his arm wrapped around her tiny neck. "I told you what I'd do," he seethed in anger.

"Mama! Alice!" Martha screamed.

"Damn you, girl!" Joseph said. With the knife still firmly in his grip, he contemplated plunging it deep into her side or slicing her throat, but those were empty threats. While he was a monster by all definitions, murdering children was where he drew the line.

"Mama!" Martha hollered.

Angered, Joseph cocked his arm back and came back down with the hilt of his knife against the back of Martha's head.

Martha yelped then dropped to the floor unconscious. On her way down, her hand got tangled with Joseph's pocket watch chain and ripped it from his vest.

Unaware that his watch had fallen out, and knowing he needed to get upstairs fast, Joseph stepped over Martha and sprinted in the direction of the stairs.

In her room, hearing the chaos and terrified for her life, Alice went to her window and opened it. The cool air washed across her flushed face. She went to climb out but paused; she looked back to her door and questioned whether she should run or go help. She'd heard Martha crying out for help, but the idea of going out and challenging whomever it was seemed impossible. Unable to come to grips with just running away, Alice abandoned the idea and headed for the door. Before opening it, she took a knitting needle from atop her dresser and wrapped her hand around it. She threw open the door and found Joseph standing there.

"There you are!" Joseph hollered. He reached for her, but Alice went to slam the door.

Before the door could close, Joseph stuck his arm out and prevented it from closing. "Let me in."

Alice did what came naturally. With the needle firmly in her grasp, she recoiled and slammed it into Joseph's arm.

He wailed in pain and pulled his arm back, allowing Alice to close the door. With nowhere to go but out, Alice raced to the window, climbed out onto the eave, then jumped the twelve feet to the ground below.

Joseph kicked the door in. He stepped inside but didn't see her. He first went to the bed and looked under, but she wasn't there; then he noticed the window was open. He ran to it, looked out, but couldn't see her. "I'll find you!" he hollered.

Alice didn't look back after hitting the ground. She sprinted for the open field and ran across it at breakneck speed. When she was hundreds of yards away, she stopped and looked back to the house. She prayed everyone was safe, but she just knew that wasn't the case. Unsure where to go, she headed to the one place she thought she'd find safety: the woods. After what seemed like an eternity, she took refuge in a hollowed-out dead tree. She covered herself in dead dry leaves, waited, and prayed, not just for her family but also that they wouldn't find her.

MISSOULA, MONTANA

Billy held the telegram from Coeur d'Alene, his mouth wide open in shock at what was written on the paper. "Look at this," he said, handing the telegram to Hemsworth, who was anxious to read it.

Glancing over it, Hemsworth said, "Apparently they don't know or won't tell us."

"We should demand they give us an answer."

"Demand? My young friend, we're deputy marshals. We don't make demands unless you're a wanted criminal; otherwise we don't have much power or leverage."

"But they owe us some sort of explanation," Billy pressed.

Crumpling up the paper and tossing it in a trash can, Hemsworth gave Billy a smile and said, "No, they don't, and when or if we ever end up sitting behind a desk like they do back in Idaho, then we'll be able to know privileged information and withhold it all we want."

"You're just going to let this go?" Billy asked in a righteous tone.

"I am. Listen, Billy, we take orders from those in authority and arrest outlaws; if they felt we needed to know, I suspect they would tell us," Hemsworth said, putting his hat on. He turned and headed from the telegraph office's exit.

"Where are you going?"

"To the marshal's office to get Bob, or Alfred; I'll never get use to calling him Alfred," Hemsworth joked.

Billy followed Hemsworth out of the office and into the bright morning light. He donned his wide-brimmed hat and said, "When we're done with this job, the first thing I'm going to do when we get back to Coeur d'Alene is see Bradley." Bradley was the United States Marshal for their district and their direct boss.

"I'd recommend you don't do that. It's unfortunate, but we have to deal with politics in this profession, and if you have a desire to advance someday, you'd be wise to keep your mouth shut."

"I'm aware of the politics, but this entire thing with Bob is just off. I smell a rat, you could say," Billy said.

"I agree, but there's something clearly sensitive, and I'm betting it has something to do with Canada. By the way, I'm quite sure the Canadians will serve him the justice he so rightly deserves."

"I pray you're right."

The men reached the marshal's office, but before stepping inside, Hemsworth turned to Billy and said, "I know it's hard, but don't take this job personally."

"How can you not?"

"Let me clarify, don't let your emotions dictate your actions when it comes to this job."

"I'll always follow my heart as well as my mind; they work well together," Billy said.

"Just think bigger is all I'm saying. I know we're both upset that Bob is not getting the justice he deserves here for the murder of the marshal, but he will get justice, period, just not here."

"Well, I hope you're right," Billy said, unconvinced, as he suspected something wasn't right.

"Now come on, let's get ole Bob and head north; the sooner this is over, the better," Hemsworth said.

TWO MILES SOUTH OF GREAT FALLS, MONTANA

The dog rubbed its wet and cold nose against Alice's face and sniffed. He smelled her for a second then began to lick her cheeks.

After a few wet licks, Alice opened her eyes and recoiled at the sight of the large mastiff.

The dog also jumped back, cocked its head, and gave Alice a curious look.

Alice squinted from the bright morning light and gazed around but didn't see anyone. Sitting up, she brushed off the leaves that covered her and took in her surroundings. The sun was up, which meant she'd been sleeping for more than a few hours. Her mind raced to the events from earlier. She hopped to her feet and looked around to get her bearings.

The dog didn't budge; it stood staring at her.

"Where do I go, boy?" she asked the dog.

The dog answered her with a deep bark.

"You're a pretty boy," she said, petting the dog's head. She glanced around until she felt confident of the direction she should travel. With concern and fear of what she'd find upon returning home, she headed through the woods with urgency.

***

She reached the edge of the woods and saw her house in the distance. The trip through the dense woods felt like it had taken an eternity, when in reality she'd only spent ten minutes traveling. Before stepping out into the field, she looked for anything out of place but saw nothing that would tell her if the men were still there or not.

Assuming they had gone, she broke the protection

and cover of the tree line and stepped into the open field. She paused and looked again, but still she didn't see anything that would tell her the situation at the house. With nothing to go on and a need to see her family, she sprinted towards the house.

She reached the edge of the field. The house was now thirty feet away. Again she looked around but saw nothing out of sorts. Just as she was about to take a step, the front door opened and out came Anne, her grandmother.

Anne went to the rocker she always sat in and took a seat.

As if nothing had happened, Anne began to rock back and forth.

Feeling safe, Alice exited the field and crossed the yard. "Grandma!" she cried out.

Anne's eyes widened upon hearing her name being called. She looked around until she spotted Alice. "My dear, where have you been?"

Alice stopped and asked, "Are they gone?"

"Yes, they're gone," Anne said.

Sighing, Alice ran onto the porch and embraced Anne. Tears flowed as she said, "Are you okay? Is Mama? What about Martha? I heard her cry out last night."

"My dear, things will forever be different, but the worst of it is now over," Anne said, attempting to bring solace to Alice's concerns.

"Where's Martha?"

"She's upstairs resting. She's been through a lot."

"Did they?" Alice asked, praying that they hadn't

raped her.

"Oh no, they didn't do what you're thinking to her. Those men are cruel and despicable, but they still had enough morals left in them that prevented them from doing that."

"And Mama?"

"She's resting too. She had a rough night," Anne said.

Alice pulled back and asked, "And you, Grandma?"

"I'm fine. I didn't get to be this old by being soft."

Noting the bruises on Anne's face and hands finally, Alice said, "They hurt you."

"It's nothing. Now go check on your mama and sister; don't worry about me," Anne said, nudging her to go inside.

"Shouldn't we notify the sheriff?"

"We're not doing anything," Maggie blared from the open front door, startling Alice.

Stunned by her mother's comment, Alice said, "But those men, they...they hurt you and Grandma."

"Those men do what men do, and now they're gone. We won't be involving any lawmen, who will just make assumptions and such," Maggie said as she slowly walked out of the house. She lowered herself carefully into a rocker chair next to Anne and continued, "I see you ran away."

"I didn't know what else to do," Alice replied, her tone defensive.

"That was smart," Maggie said.

"But I did try. I went to go help, but—"

"Girl, what would you have done? Nothing, that's what. You would have just ended up…" Maggie snapped before cutting herself off.

Alice went to her mother's side and took her hand. "We need to tell the law. We must; those men need to go to jail or should be hanged for what they did."

Maggie pulled her hand away and glared at Alice. "Damn it, ain't nothing going to happen to those men. I knew they were trouble the second I heard them ride up. I could smell it on them. Thing is, that's how most men are; you can't trust 'em, nope."

"But Pa wasn't like that," Alice said.

"Your pa was a special man, but don't think he didn't act crazy now and then," Maggie said.

"But he wouldn't have ever done that," Alice barked.

"You're right, but most men would if given the opportunity. You can't trust men, you hear me, Alice, do ya?"

"But—"

"Do you hear me?" Maggie shouted.

Lowering her head, Alice answered, "Yes, Ma."

"Now go fetch me some whiskey," Maggie said.

"No, Ma, don't start drinking. It's still morning," Alice pleaded.

"Go do what your ma says," Anne said softly.

Alice didn't say a word; the look of deep sadness and despair was written on her dirt-smudged face.

"Go get me my whiskey," Maggie barked, glaring at Alice.

Alice's sympathy for her mother instantly melted

away. She growled under her breath and marched into the house. In the kitchen she found the whiskey and went to head back outside to deliver it when she heard Martha whimpering in the other room. Needing to see her sister, she walked into the living room, to find her on the love seat, her face buried in the palms of her hands. "Why are you crying?"

"It was horrible," Martha cried, her voice muffled.

Alice sat next to her. Draping her arm over Martha's shoulder, she squeezed and said, "I'm sorry you had to experience that."

"They hurt Mama and Grandma," Martha whined.

"I know."

Looking up, she asked, "Where were you? Why didn't you help us?"

Taken aback by Martha's questions, Alice replied, "I tried but barely escaped myself."

"Do you think they'll return?"

"They may."

"I miss Papa. This wouldn't have happened if he were alive," Martha said.

"I think you're right, but we have to face the fact he's gone," Alice replied. "What did they do to you?"

"He grabbed me really hard and dragged me from the outhouse. Then he struck me in the head. I woke up later and found Mama and Grandma upstairs, but the men were gone."

Alice examined the top of Martha's head but stopped when Martha cried out in pain.

Recoiling from Alice, Martha snapped, "Ouch, that

hurts."

"Sorry, I was just seeing how bad they hit you."

"The hit split open my head. It's not too bad, but it does hurt," Martha explained.

"Did anyone take a look to see if you need stitches?"

"Yes, Mama looked and said I'd be fine."

"Where's my whiskey?" Maggie hollered from outside.

"I'd best go deliver Mama her medicine," Alice quipped.

"Can we play a game when you return?" Martha asked.

Petting Martha's hand gently, Alice said, "Of course, whatever you'd like to do, but first could I get cleaned up?"

"Sure," Martha said. "Where did you go?"

"The woods, I went and hid in that old dead oak," Alice said.

"I'm sorry," Martha whimpered.

Taking her hand in hers, Alice asked, "What could you feel sorry for?"

"I should have warned everyone sooner or maybe fought back," Martha said, tears streaming down her cheeks.

Alice wiped the tears away with her hand, lifted Martha's chin, and looked deeply into her green eyes. "You're very brave for what you did. Few people would have cried out; I heard you. You did try to warn us and you suffered for it. I'm just so grateful they didn't hurt you worse."

"Where's my damn whiskey?" Maggie hollered again.

Wiping her eyes, Martha said, "I'm also sorry I sounded mad at you."

"Oh, it's okay, we're all a bit emotional right now," Alice said sweetly.

"You'd best go before Ma comes in here and gives you a good smack," Martha said.

"You're right," Alice said. She stood and smoothed out her soiled and wrinkled skirt.

"I overheard them saying we're not going to tell the law. I don't understand."

"I don't either, but we don't have a choice in the matter."

"If I were older, I'd saddle a horse and ride after those evil men," Martha said.

"And what would you do if you caught them?"

"I'd put a bullet in them, one each, right between the eyes," Martha growled.

Shocked by her response, Alice said, "You know, little sister, that's not a bad idea. Those men need killing so they won't do to someone else what they did here."

"How about we go?" Martha asked.

"I don't think so," Alice said, quickly dismissing the fantasy.

Maggie appeared in the room suddenly. She hobbled over to Alice and snatched the bottle from her hands. "Darn, girl, don't you listen?"

"I was coming, Mama," Alice said.

"I heard what you two were saying, and it's not going to happen. If you got some wild hair to go ride off after those men, you'd only end up dead yourself," Maggie said. She pulled the cork from the bottle and took a swig. Wiping her mouth, she continued, "Now get yourself upstairs, Alice, and get cleaned up. And you, stop your crying and sniveling. What happened last night is over. Think of it as a lesson, nothing more. Know that you two can't trust men; many are scoundrels like those men last night."

"But, Mama, why not tell the sheriff so he can arrest those men?" Martha asked.

"On account that I don't want the sheriff knowing what happened. People like to talk, and I can't have rumors circulating about me and especially you girls. I know I've not been the best mother since your pa died, but I do care about how people think about you," Maggie said.

Once her mother revealed the real reason for not informing the sheriff, Alice could understand; yet she wanted those men to pay for what they did. Seeing them hang would actually bring her joy even though she'd never witnessed a hanging before.

"Now get your hindquarters upstairs and get cleaned up and, you, go prepare us some food; your grandma and me are hungry," Maggie barked.

Alice nodded and went upstairs while Martha wiped the final tears from her cheeks and eyes, then headed for the kitchen.

At the top of the stairs, Alice turned and looked back down to find her mother taking a large drink from the bottle. The sight filled her with disgust, but there wasn't a thing she could do about it. Her mother was her mother. If she knew how to bring back the woman she'd known before, she'd try, but right now she was clueless about how to do that.

FIVE MILES SOUTHWEST OF GREAT FALLS, MONTANA

Harry rubbed his sore and bruised wrists; his thoughts were no doubt torn about what he should do about his partners. He wasn't like them; in fact, he couldn't be more opposite.

They had come back like they promised, but he was finding it hard to forgive them. He didn't have to ask what had transpired at the house, as they gloated about their depraved actions.

He watched as the three bathed at the edge of the Missouri River. Like small boys, they splashed water and played.

Throwing his soaked shirt at Harry, Joseph joked, "C'mon, Harry, don't act so bent out of shape."

Angered by the childish act, Harry tossed the shirt in the mud and spat, "Look at you. You just got done doing all sorts of inhumane acts, and now you're playing like a damn child."

"Oh, you're just sore. Get over it," Joseph sneered. "Look at him; he's acting all high and mighty when in reality he's the one being a child and pouting."

"Can you hurry up? We're no doubt behind schedule," Harry said.

"We're fine. We'll get him when we get him," Gus barked. He took a mouthful of water and spit it out like a fountain.

"I'm going to ride into town," Harry said.

"What town?" Joseph asked.

"Great Falls," Harry said.

"For what?" Joseph asked, concerned.

"They told us to stop and check for any wires that may come in. I figure Great Falls is the closest, and now that we're behind schedule, we should see if anything has changed," Harry said, fully knowing there was risk in doing so.

"Shouldn't we be riding away from Great Falls?" Henry asked.

"We should be riding away from town, but I'm not responsible for anything you fools did. We need to see if there's a telegram for us, so I'm going into town," Harry declared.

"You're such a rule follower," Joseph said mockingly.

"How many times do I have to remind you that we're here to do a job, not play around or rape women," Harry barked angrily. "We're getting paid good money for this, and I'd like to get home to my family as soon as possible."

Joseph strutted out of the water and sat down on a rock. He looked at his arm and squeezed the wound from Alice's knitting needle. Blood oozed out and dripped onto his foot.

Harry scowled at Joseph and said, "You got hurt?"

"Just a minor thing. Say, did I ever tell you I was married once?" Joseph asked.

Harry couldn't care less about Joseph's life and didn't reply.

"She's a nice girl; she had a lot of plans for us, specifically for me. I don't take kindly to being told how to live. I left one day and never returned," Joseph said.

"You were married?" Henry asked, still in the water bathing.

"Yep, you heard right. That seems like two lifetimes ago now," Joseph said.

"You never mentioned you'd been married before," Gus said, walking out of the water and sitting on a large rock near the water's edge, his long underwear sopping wet.

"I don't talk about it much," Joseph said.

"You're still married. It doesn't just end because you don't return home," Harry said.

"You sure?" Joseph asked.

"I'm pretty sure. You're just estranged from your wife is all," Harry said.

"Estranged? What does that mean? I still write her now and then and even send her money on account I feel guilty for leaving her, so I'm not strange," Joseph replied.

"Estranged, not strange," Harry said, shaking his head at how uneducated his partners were.

"I'm pretty sure I'm not married anymore though," Joseph said.

"Did you ever get a divorce decree?" Harry asked.

"No," Joseph answered. He shrugged off Harry's

complaints and continued, "She even took some of the money I sent her and got herself a little farm in Moscow."

"Where's Moscow?" Gus asked.

"Idaho," Joseph replied.

Unable to let go the small details, Harry snapped, "If you didn't get a decree, you're still married, you dolt."

"Just shut your mouth or I'll tie you up again," Joseph said.

"Was she a looker?" Gus asked Joseph.

"Oh yeah, last letter I got from her a few years back, she begged for me to return to her and said that she'd moved to a nice little farm in Idaho. Poor Melissa thinks I'll join her there."

Henry finished up and exited the water. Like the other two, he found a rock and sat down. "Say, before this job, what were you doing, Gus?"

"Oh, jobs here and there," Gus replied.

"And you, Harry?" Henry asked.

"Worked at a sawmill before it closed down," Harry said, his tone still showing his aggravation with the others.

"You, Joe?" Henry asked.

"Similar to Gus," Joseph said.

"That's right, you two knew each other before," Henry said.

"I met Joseph three months ago. We've been riding together since," Gus said.

"What did you do before that?" Henry asked Joe.

Sitting up, Joe snapped, "Enough of the damn fool questions."

Henry recoiled from the response. "I was just curious."

"Curious like a damn fool woman, always asking questions, wanting to get to know you more. Well, I don't care to share," Joseph said. He hopped to his feet, grabbed his underwear, and slipped them on. "We're going with you."

"You want to go into town even though there might be a posse looking for you?" Harry asked, shocked that Joseph seemed unconcerned.

"There ain't no posse looking for us," Joseph said.

"And how do you know that?" Harry asked, finding it hard to believe.

"On account those women never got a look at us, and for the fact that I told the mother that if anyone muttered a damn word, I'd come back and kill her precious children. I always found a credible threat to be a good deterrent."

"And you really think your threats will be heeded?" Harry asked.

"What if you're wrong?" Henry asked.

"Henry's right," Gus said.

"Don't be cowards. Get your clothes on; we ride into town," Joseph said. He picked up his trousers and pulled them on, followed by his shirt and vest. When he began to button his vest, he noticed his watch was missing. Startled, he looked all around on the ground around him but didn't find it. "Have any of you seen my watch?"

"I didn't know you had a watch," Henry said.

"You lost your father's gold watch?" Gus asked. He

knew about the watch and knew just how much Joseph cherished it.

Frantic now, Joseph traced his path to the water, his eyes scanning the ground. "No, no, no."

"Maybe you left it at the house," Harry snarled.

"If I did, I'm riding back to get it," Joseph said, making his way to his horse.

"No, we're not going back to the house," Harry snapped.

"If I can't find my watch, I damn sure am," Joseph said.

"This time I agree with Harry. We're not going back to the house, and I suggest you don't do it either. It was just an old watch. After this job you'll be able to buy yourself a new one," Gus said.

"You know how much I love that watch," Joseph barked as he searched around the hitched horses.

"Joe, I'm with Gus and Harry. It would be a mistake to go back to the house. I don't think we'd get two feet without getting shot," Henry said. "Plus those women are tough. You threatened to kill them, and they never gave up where they had any money hidden away. If we go back now, they'll put holes in us." He slipped on his trousers and sauntered to his horse.

"Joseph, the other fellas are right. It's risky enough for us to be riding into town, but to have you going back to that house on a hunch, that's too much for us to agree to. If you left the watch there, count it as the price paid for that night."

"Damn it!" Joseph yelled as he continued his search.

"It's just a watch," Gus said.

"No, it's not, it's not just a watch. It has…" Joseph said before cutting himself off.

"It has?" Harry asked.

"Nothing, never mind," Joseph said. He grunted his displeasure then kicked a rock.

Gus and Henry arrived at the horses.

"If there is a posse looking out for you all, we'd best get going now," Harry said.

All dressed from their swim, Harry and Henry climbed onto their horses. Gus pulled his horse around to face Joseph, who stood next to his with his head resting against the saddle. "What's the matter?"

Shaking his head, Joseph said, "Nothing is the matter. That watch meant a lot to me." He got on his horse and took the reins. "I'm gonna get that watch back, I promise you. One day, I'll go back and get that watch."

TWO MILES SOUTH OF GREAT FALLS, MONTANA

Martha held out her hand, and in it was a gold pocket watch.

Alice stared at it and said, "You took it from him?"

Martha nodded.

"Can I see it?"

Martha again nodded.

Alice picked up the watch. She ran her thumb across the glass face. Seeing the time on it, she glanced up at the clock on their wall and confirmed it was not set right. "I think it needs to be wound." She turned the crown until it stopped. Examining the face, she saw the second hand begin to tick. "There, it's working," she said with a faint smile. "You have something of value for all the trouble last night." She handed the watch back to Martha.

Martha shook her head and said, "I don't want it."

"Why not? It's a gold watch; it's worth something."

"No."

"The watch is just a thing. It won't hurt you," Alice said, holding the watch out.

"No," Martha insisted.

"You really don't want it?"

"No, I don't. It's not mine, and every time I read his name on the back, I'll see his face."

"Name on the back?" Alice asked.

"Yes, it's right there," Martha said, taking the watch, flipping it over, and pointing at the back.

Alice leaned close and squinted. "Where?"

Martha pointed closer and said, "It's faint, but his name is right there."

The faint light of the day caught the watch just right and allowed her to see the name etched in the back. "I see it."

"You see, I can't keep it; he even has his name on it. I want to forget last night and forget his face; now I have to forget his name," Martha seethed, her previous sorrow replaced with a brewing anger.

"I'll hold on to it for you, then. When I have a chance, I'll sell it and give you the money. How does that sound?" Alice asked, hoping Martha would agree.

"I don't care what you do with it. I don't want to ever see it again," Martha said. She pressed her eyes closed tightly and continued, "My head hurts. I'm going to go rest."

"You're just tired is all. You should get some rest."

Martha got up and headed across the creaking floor to Alice's bedroom door.

"I love you," Alice said.

Martha stopped, turned and said, "I love you too."

"Go get some rest. We'll talk more tomorrow."

"If I get scared, can I sleep with you?"

"Of course," Alice replied, her heart aching. Poor Martha was so different than she was. In her was a tenderness, a sweet and gentle person who was now confronted with the evils of the world at such a young age. She prayed it didn't affect the rest of her life, but knew it probably would.

Martha left the bedroom, closing the door behind her.

Alone, Alice took the watch to the window to catch the last bit of daylight. She angled the watch so the sun's rays caught the etching on the back and read out loud, "Joseph Paul King."

MISSOULA, MONTANA

Billy waited outside the telegram office, atop his horse, waiting for Hemsworth, who was inside the telegram office.

Slouched in his saddle, Al snickered and sneered,

mumbling random things to Billy.

"How old are you?" Al asked.

Billy ignored Al. He was growing impatient with how long it was taking Hemsworth. They had spent the greater part of the day preparing for the journey, which they estimated would take eight days to ride at the pace they'd have to go.

Al gave Billy a glance and sneered, "So young."

"Just shut your mouth," Billy fired back. He'd heard about all he could take from Al, and the thought of beating Al senseless popped into his mind more than once.

"It's really sad, you know," Al said.

"I said shut up," Billy ordered.

Ignoring Billy, Al continued with his taunts. "Yep, very sad for such a young lad to end up six feet under. How about you just take off these shackles and let me go?" Al lifted his arms and shook; the irons clanged.

"I should take those off and beat you with them," Billy barked.

"Boy, we're not going to make it to wherever you're taking me, you gotta know that," Al said.

"You know something, Bob, or whatever your name is, I'd just as soon take you just outside town and hang you from the first tree we encounter, then tell whoever that you tried to escape and we had to put a bullet in the back of your head."

Al shook his head and began to chuckle. "You really don't know the mess you're in, do ya?"

"Why don't you enlighten me?" Billy said, trotting

over next to Al. He grimaced upon looking at his deeply bruised face. "Damn, the butt of my rifle did a number on your noggin."

"I'll pay you back for that too once I'm out of these irons here," Al said, again shaking the shackles vigorously.

Billy leaned forward on the saddle horn and whispered, "Keep running your piehole and I'll put another hole in your damn forehead."

"You really don't know who I am, do you?" Al asked.

Curious about the statement made by Al, Billy declared, "Why don't you tell me?"

Al's eyes widened. "You don't, do you?"

Hemsworth exited the telegram office, a piece of paper in his hand. "This keeps getting odder by the moment."

"What did it say?" Billy asked.

Hemsworth went to reply but stopped short when he caught Al leaning forward to listen. "Come closer."

Billy trotted over to Hemsworth and lowered his head.

Whispering, Hemsworth said, "They gave us a specific route to take, and get this, they want us to stop in Great Falls. There, we'll receive another telegram telling us where to go next."

"I've never heard of such a thing," Billy said, ensuring to keep his voice down.

"Me either, but I suppose there's a first for everything," Hemsworth said.

"And nothing else? What are they thinking back in

Idaho?" Billy asked.

"This telegram wasn't from our office in Idaho. This came from the United States Attorney's office in San Francisco," Hemsworth said.

"Damn it, Eric, something is off about this, I'm telling you; I don't like it, not one bit," Billy growled.

"I hear ya, but we need to keep our heads down and do what we're told," Hemsworth said. He folded the paper and shoved it in his inside jacket pocket. He looked to the sky and said, "An hour before it's dark; let's get on our way and get a few hours' ride in before we bed down for the night."

"Good idea. The sooner we're done with him and this entire situation, the better I'll feel," Billy said.

Hemsworth strode to his horse and mounted it. As he settled into the saddle, the leather creaking as he did, Al began to laugh. Looking over his shoulder, Hemsworth asked, "What do you find so humorous?"

"That I'm looking at two dead men and they don't even know it." Al chuckled.

"Dead men?" Hemsworth asked.

"Don't listen to him. He's been saying mindless things since you walked into the telegraph office," Billy said.

"I thought this young one was ignorant; now I see you are too," Al said.

Hemsworth pulled his horse around until it was side by side with Al's. "Now why would you be so rude? You do know we're escorting you across some rough terrain; there's no sayin' what might happen."

"Now that is humorous. You're not going to do anything to me, nothin'," Al spat.

"I've had to use everything in my power to talk my partner down from killing you, so I'd suggest you keep your mouth closed and show some respect," Hemsworth said.

"Marshal, are you a gambling man?" Al asked.

"I wager now and then," Hemsworth replied.

"Good, how about making a wager with me?" Al said.

Disgusted by Al's contempt, Billy shook his head.

"And what would this wager be about?" Hemsworth asked.

"On when you two die. I say it will be in...two days. Yep, two days from now I'll be looking down on your corpses."

Hemsworth rolled his eyes and trotted away from Al.

"Is that a no?" Al asked.

"Al, are you going to be talking the entire time we ride?" Hemsworth asked.

"I do like to have conversation. My mother always said I was a talker," Al answered.

Hemsworth shot Billy a look and nodded.

Knowing exactly what he wanted, Billy said, "Gladly." He rode up alongside Al, pulled out a handkerchief, and stuffed it into Al's mouth.

Al shook his head and tried to spit out the handkerchief, but Billy took out another from his saddlebag, wrapped it around Al's face, and secured it tightly. Al's eyes bulged in anger and he squirmed in the saddle.

"If you get too jumpy, you'll fall out of the saddle. Then we'll have to tie a rope around you and pull you along on foot," Billy warned with a smile.

Al mumbled loudly.

"Please fall off the horse, please," Billy said.

"Al, he's right. If you get out of line, I'll have you walk the next few hours," Hemsworth warned.

Taking the men seriously, Al settled down. He shot Billy a hard look and mumbled something unintelligible.

Smiling ear to ear, Billy said, "Peace and quiet."

"You ready?" Hemsworth asked.

"I am," Billy said.

CHAPTER FOUR

JULY 10, 1895

TWO MILES SOUTH OF GREAT FALLS, MONTANA

"Alice, get down here now!" Maggie bellowed from the front room of the house.

In her room, Alice heard her mother's call and sighed. She could hear an angry tone in her mother's voice, and it could only mean one thing: she was out of whiskey.

"Alice, get down here this instant!" Maggie barked from the bottom of the stairs.

"Coming!" Alice replied. She put her book down and went to her bedroom door. She paused when she saw the watch sitting on her nightstand. Her mind went to Martha, and she was curious as to why she hadn't slept with her like she'd hinted she wanted to do.

"Alice!" Maggie shrieked.

Throwing open the door, Alice snapped back, "I'm coming, Ma."

"Why don't you answer when I call out the first time, huh?" Maggie sneered.

"I did; you just didn't hear me," Alice said, racing down the stairs.

"Don't give me sass, girl," Maggie said, clenching Alice's forearm. She squeezed and said, "Where's your sister?"

"If she's not down here, then I suppose she's still in bed. I haven't seen her since waking," Alice answered.

"Damn girl sleeps all the time," Maggie complained.

"Ma, what do you want?"

"I need you to go into town and get some items."

"Let me guess, whiskey is one of them?" Alice snarked.

Maggie cocked her hand back but stopped short of striking Alice. "Don't be smart with me."

"Go ahead, Ma, hit me. Soon I'll be eighteen and I'll hit you back," Alice threatened.

Stunned by Alice's sharp response, Maggie said, "You ain't eighteen yet, and no matter what your age, you don't sass your mother."

Alice sneered and thought to herself that Maggie was the furthest thing from actually being a mother.

"You know where the money is. Go to the merc and get a pound of flour, a half-pound of pork belly, and a half-dozen eggs. Then go to Singer's and get me two bottles; you know what I like."

Alice nodded.

"Now go, hurry. I want to make some beans for dinner."

"You're making dinner?" Alice asked, surprised.

"Girl, you're this close to getting a beating," Maggie said, holding up two fingers.

Alice sauntered to the kitchen and pulled out the tin

that held what money the family had. She fished through it and took out what she'd need. She pocketed it and headed out the front. There she saw Anne sitting in her chair, rocking back and forth. "Good morning, Grandma."

"Good mornin', doll face. Where's your little sister?" Anne asked.

"Still sleeping, I think," Alice replied. "I'm off to town. Do you need anything?"

"I'm fine. Be safe."

Maggie appeared with a small-framed revolver in her hand. She extended her hand with the pistol in it, the grip facing Alice. "Take this with you."

"You want me to take Pa's old pistol?" Alice asked. She'd never ridden to town armed before, but after what had transpired, she welcomed the ability to carry a weapon.

"Go ahead, take it. One can never be too safe," Maggie said.

Alice took the pistol, admired it for a second, then slipped it into a pocket on her skirt. "Thank you, Ma."

"See, your ma ain't so mean, is she?" Anne asked.

Alice replied with a simple smile. "I'll be back as soon as I can."

"Don't dawdle," Maggie said.

"I won't, Ma, I promise," Alice said, turned and raced towards the barn.

LINCOLN, MONTANA

Billy glanced back to see Al leering at him. "Hot damn, if looks could kill, I'd be dead as a doornail."

Hemsworth craned his head back and chuckled. "You aren't joking."

"I don't think Al likes us much," Billy quipped as he lifted his head to the sky and soaked up the sun's warm rays. "Ah, feels good."

Al mumbled through the gag they kept him in. Every time they removed it for him to eat or drink, he'd immediately start swearing and making threats. Unable and unwilling to listen to him, they just kept the gag in his mouth.

"I bet he didn't get a good night's sleep last night," Billy said with a snicker.

"Being tied to a boulder, sitting up, with your handkerchief stuffed in his mouth doesn't make for comfortable conditions," Hemsworth said.

"Say, how far till Great Falls?"

"Another day."

"How do you do it?" Billy asked.

"Do what?"

"Stay married, yet be gone all the time?"

"It's a careful balance, but my wife met me when I was already a marshal, so she's used to this life. I bring in a good wage, and she lives nicely compared to most. She's not a needy woman and has grown quite accustomed to me being gone. Heck, I think when I come home now, I get in her way," Hemsworth said.

Billy nodded as he took in all the information.

"What's with the question about my marriage?" Hemsworth asked.

"Just curious," Billy said.

"I suppose you'll want to get hitched one of these days."

"One day."

"Say, what happened back—"

"If you're going to ask me about that night with the whore, I don't want to talk about it," Billy fired back, his casual demeanor now gone.

"You can tell me. I'm your partner and I like to think I'm also a good friend."

"I don't like whores," Billy spat.

"I understand that, but why the visceral reaction?"

"On account that I don't like them."

Hemsworth pulled back on his reins and stopped his horse. "Just tell me, for Christ's sake."

"You want to know why?"

"Yeah, I would, only because I'd like to know my friend."

"I happen to respect women, and I think that prostitution doesn't honor them. They're objectified and abused. I think it's degrading," Billy snapped.

Taken aback by Billy's forceful rebuttal, Hemsworth asked, "Have you ever been with a woman before?"

Shocked by the question, Billy trotted ahead, pulling Al's horse along with him.

As Al rode by Hemsworth, he saw a shit-eating grin on Al's face. Knowing he had asked a deeply personal question, Hemsworth rode up alongside Billy and said, "Please accept my apology for that stupid question."

"What does it matter if I've been with a woman or not? I'm a good man, I treat all good and decent people with respect, and I think highly of the fairer sex. Why is my behavior or lack of a certain type of behavior now subject to mockery?"

"I wasn't mocking you," Hemsworth said defensively. He wished he'd just kept his mouth shut now, but it was difficult on these long rides.

"It sure sounded like it."

"I've just never seen you act that way towards prostitutes...actually I've never seen you ever interact with one until then," Hemsworth said. He thought about the years they'd been riding together, and it was true: Billy never talked to or gave any attention to prostitutes.

"I like women, real women, not ones who sell their bodies and do vile things," Billy said.

"My friend, I do apologize. I meant nothing wrong. I was just curious."

"I don't want to bed a whore. I wish to find a good, decent woman, get married, and have a family. Why is that so bad?"

"It's not, it's not at all," Hemsworth said.

Al could be heard chuckling behind his gag.

Billy stopped his horse, shot Al a harsh look, and barked, "Shut it."

Al continued to chuckle, knowing it annoyed Billy.

Not hesitating to lash out, Billy pulled his horse back alongside Al's and slapped him across the face, toppling him from the saddle and onto the hard ground.

Al hit with a thump and began to holler.

"Did you have to do that?" Hemsworth asked.

"Yeah, I did."

"Get him up."

"You get him up," Billy fired back.

Hemsworth raised his brow and said, "As your superior, I'm giving you an order. I understand you didn't like my personal question, but that doesn't give you permission to defy an order from me."

Billy hopped from his saddle, grabbed Al forcibly, and pulled him to his feet. He got him back in the saddle and said, "There."

"I don't think we've ever had a fight."

Straddling his horse, Billy said, "There's a first for everything." He took the reins of Al's horse and trotted ahead.

Hemsworth shook his head as he thought about the incident and said, "Note to self, never ever mention prostitutes to Billy again."

TWO MILES SOUTH OF GREAT FALLS, MONTANA

Alice enjoyed the sojourn into town; it was nice seeing people and things. She didn't do exactly what her mother would have wanted, as she took time to enjoy and tinker with all sorts of items in the mercantile store.

She longed for turning eighteen, pledging to herself that she'd leave and go find a new life. However, her thoughts of freedom did leave her with guilt, as leaving was all but abandoning Martha to the hardships and emotional turmoil of their mother.

She thought of taking Martha with her, but where would they go, and how would she support them both? Of course, she contemplated staying until Martha turned older, but her selfishness always won the debate. It wasn't her fault her sister was her age, and was Martha really her responsibility? Of course, the practical answer was no, but her heart would scream out for Martha. It didn't matter that Martha was only her sister; she did feel a deep responsibility for her care and well-being since Maggie wasn't truly a mother.

As she made her way around a turn, her house came into view. She slowed and looked to make sure it was safe to approach. Seeing no horses or anything out of place, she advanced farther. When she made the turn off the road and onto the long drive, a loud scream followed by what could only be described as wailing came from inside the house. She pulled back on the reins, forcing the horse to stop. She looked but saw nothing. She then ceased her breathing and listened.

Nothing.

Fear rose in her. Were the men back? Had someone else come to take advantage?

The wails again reverberated from the house.

This time she could tell it was her mother's voice.

The front door opened and out stepped Anne. She hobbled over to her rocking chair and sat down. In her right hand was a handkerchief. She brought it to her face and dabbed tears that were streaming from her eyes.

Cries of agony once more came from the house.

It was clearly evident something was wrong, but what? She saw her grandma and heard her mother; the one person she hadn't seen or heard from was Martha. Was she okay?

Frantic that something had happened to Martha, Alice whipped the reins against the horse's back.

The horse reared slightly and lurched forward.

Alice whipped the horse repeatedly to drive it faster. She sped down the drive and pulled up to the front of the house.

Anne looked at Alice and began to sob.

"Grandma, what's happened?" Alice asked, jumping from the wagon.

"It's your sister, dear."

Alice sprinted onto the porch and in through the open doorway of the house.

Maggie's cries of sorrow came from upstairs.

Her heart beating fast, Alice raced towards her mother's voice. Up the stairs she went and into Martha's bedroom.

"She's gone. My baby girl is gone," Maggie shrieked upon seeing Alice in the doorway.

Shocked, Alice took a few steps into the room but stopped when she saw Martha's small body lying motionless on the bed, her skin opaque. "What happened?"

In between sobs, Maggie answered, "After, ah, after you left, ah, I came up. She, ah, your sister, she, ah, was just lying here as you see now."

"What do you mean?" Alice asked, still frozen in place only a few feet in the room.

"I don't know, you left and, ah, I found her like this," Maggie said. She crawled up alongside Martha's body and wrapped her arms around her still body.

Alice took a few more steps into the room. She was now a foot from the bed. "But how?"

"I don't know."

"But I talked to her just last night. She, she told me she might come to my room if she got scared, but she never showed. I thought she had fallen asleep. I don't understand how this could have happened," Alice said. "Are you sure?"

Maggie shot Alice an angry stare and snapped, "Of course I know. My poor baby's body is cold and stiff. She must have died last night or early this morning."

"But from what? I don't understand. She was fine last night. How could she just die?"

"I can only assume that this is God's judgment for my sins," Maggie cried.

Alice found the courage and pushed past her mother to get next to Martha's body.

"What are you doing?" Maggie cried out.

"I'm looking her over," Alice said. She ran her hands over Martha's body, looking for anything that looked suspicious. She rolled her onto her side, but her head remained stuck to the pillow. She examined there and saw that her hair was stuck due to blood that had seeped from the wound on her head. Alice carefully looked and saw the gash in her head was far worse than she had been told. "Ma, I think she died from the hit to the head."

"How can that be?" Maggie asked, her entire body trembling.

Laying Martha's body back and folding her arms over her chest tenderly, Alice replied, "It must have caused slow bleeding in her head. I'm not a doctor, so I don't know."

"It's my fault, all mine," Maggie sobbed.

"Ma, stop crying. It's not your fault. Those men did this. They killed Martha," Alice snapped.

"No, no, it was because of the person I've become. I lost your father, and I, I couldn't handle it. I took my pain out on you and Martha. I'm being punished for that," Maggie cried.

"No, Ma, it was those men who did this. You need to go into town and tell the sheriff."

"I can't, no."

"Why? Why can't you go tell the sheriff?"

"Because it's my fault, that's why!" Maggie roared.

"It's not, those men came and did this. In fact, one man specifically hit Martha in the head; that's what killed her."

Unable to stand any longer on her wobbly legs, Maggie sat on the edge of the bed. She put her face in her hands and cried. "I'm a horrible person."

"If you won't go, then I will," Alice declared.

"And tell them what? Huh? I barely even know what they look like, and my reputation since your father died has not been good. The sheriff will question if I didn't lure those men here," Maggie said.

"What are you talking about?"

"Your ma made some big mistakes after your father died," Anne said from the doorway, startling the other two.

"I don't understand," Alice said.

Anne slowly walked into the room and sat next to Maggie. She took her hand into hers and said, "Your ma is a good woman, and I know it's hard for you to see that, considering how she's been since your pa died, but deep down, she's still that mother who loved you for so many years."

"I remember, but you're not answering my question," Alice said.

"After your pa died, she went to town to get some supplies. In her pain she ended up at a bar. I don't remember the name and it doesn't matter. After more than a few drinks, she did some things with some men that she doesn't quite remember."

Alice searched her thoughts and now remembered the time her mother didn't come back from town when she was supposed to. She recalled how Anne had gone looking for her and came back hours later. "Was it..."

"If you're thinking about the time I took Red and rode into town, yes, that time," Anne said. Red was one of their horses.

A surge of sympathy crashed over Alice upon hearing the real reason her mother was sensitive about talking to the sheriff. She dropped to her knees and took Maggie's other hand. "I didn't know, Ma."

"It's not your place to know these dark things, and now this has happened. The sheriff won't believe me. He'll think I brought those men here; he'll say this was my fault," Maggie said.

"He won't, I promise," Alice said.

"Alice, we don't know the men's names, and my memory of that night, while vivid, is mainly of the pain. It was dark. I can't truly recall what they looked like," Maggie said.

"It's true, Alice. I can't quite see their faces either," Anne said.

"I saw one specifically; I could pick him out of a crowd," Alice said.

"You can?" Maggie asked.

"I can still see him clear as day standing in the lantern light from my room. I opened the door to my room and there he was in the hallway. He turned and came at me. I closed the door on him, but he got his arm through, but I stuck him with a knitting needle. Anyways, I saw him clear as day."

"But still, I'm sure he looks like any other man," Maggie said.

"I have something more than his description, I have his name," Alice said.

GREAT FALLS, MONTANA

Standing frozen at the doorway to the sheriff's office, Alice hesitated to go in. She had been so sure of herself the entire ride there, but when faced with the opportunity, she paused.

The door opened and there stood Sheriff Amherst. "Is that you, Alice?"

"Good day, Sheriff," Alice mumbled.

Amherst cocked his head and gave her an inquisitive look. "Is everything okay?"

"No, something horrible happened."

Stepping out of the way, Amherst motioned with his hand for Alice to step inside.

Nervously she came in and looked around the small space. Two desks sat opposite each other on the left and right, with a rifle rack mounted on the right back wall. On the left was an empty jail cell.

Amherst closed the door and gently touched Alice's shoulder. "Please take a seat," he said, pointing to a chair in front of the desk on the right.

Alice rushed to the chair and sat down.

Instead of taking a seat in his chair, Amherst sat on the edge of his desk, just inches from Alice.

Anxious, Alice fidgeted with a seam on her skirt and kept her gaze focused on the window behind the desk.

"Tell me, what troubles a pretty little thing like you?" Amherst asked.

She shot him a brief look then darted her eyes away.

"It's okay, you can tell me," he said, leaning in and touching her cheek tenderly.

She recoiled and said, "Please don't do that."

"Sorry, you look upset, and I'm trying to ease your nerves," Amherst replied defensively.

"Well, Sheriff, you're doing the opposite," Alice

declared.

Sitting upright, Amherst folded his arms and asked, "Then tell me what I can do for you?"

"We were attacked the other night," she blurted out.

"Attacked?" he asked, his brow furrowed. "Describe this attack. Where was it?"

"At our house, men came looking for shelter. Ma ran them off, but they returned hours later. They hit Martha over the head and raped Ma and Grandma."

Amherst's furrowed brow grew more intense. "Men raped your ma and grandma? Who were these men?"

"I don't know who they were, men from out of town, but I do have a name."

"And what's the name?"

"Joseph Paul King."

Amherst rubbed his chin and thought. "Never heard of him. How did you come by this name?"

"My sister got his watch, and on the back of it, his name was etched," Alice replied.

"You do know that the watch may not have belonged to the man himself?"

"But it's a start, a clue for you to follow up."

"Were the men invited to come back?"

Knowing where this was going, Alice barked, "Martha is dead!"

Amherst swallowed hard and said, "Oh my, I'm sorry to hear that. And she died because of what happened? You're sure about this?"

"Sheriff, you seem hesitant to help. Why is that? I came here because my family was attacked the other night, my sister died from her injury, and my mother and grandmother were raped; yet you have questions that seem to indicate you're suspicious of my story," Alice snapped.

"Don't get fussy with me, little lady," Amherst shot back.

"My sister is dead!" Alice barked.

"I heard you the first time," Amherst said. He stood up and walked around to his chair and sat. Taking a pencil, he asked, "What was the name?"

"Joseph Paul King," Alice replied. She watched carefully as he took down the name. "When can you send out a posse?"

A smile stretched across his rugged face. "A posse? Listen, let me investigate this, and I'll get back to you. Maybe it's best you come back in a few days. I should have something about who this Joseph Paul King is by then."

"Sheriff, those men are out there and only a day's ride out, if that. Maybe they're camped somewhere local. These men are a menace to the area and need to be apprehended."

"Don't tell me how to do my job. I was elected by the people of this county, and they trust that I carry out the law in an efficient manner," Amherst bellowed.

"These men are out there now. How come you're not asking me questions about what they look like or how many?"

"How many were there?"

"Three, although four rode up initially," Alice said.

"Can you describe them?"

"I can tell you about one of them," she said as she described Joseph. "I stabbed him in the left arm, so if you find him, he'll have a wound right about here." She pointed to her own arm to show the place she stabbed him.

"Anyone else you can describe?" Amherst asked.

"No, I can't."

He sighed and said, "Like I said, come back in a few days. If I get something sooner, I'll head out to you."

"But, Sheriff, those men are close by. You should go looking for them now," Alice pressed.

"I need to investigate first," he insisted.

"Investigate what? My sister is dead and—"

"I know what you said. I need to make sure of all the facts first," he clarified.

"What facts?"

"How do I know these men weren't invited to come to your house?"

"Invited? By whom?"

He leaned back in his chair, his weight making it creak. "You're not aware, but your mother has a reputation for…how do I say this politely?"

"You disgust me, you know that?" she spat, standing up and giving him a death stare.

"I'm disgusting?" He laughed.

"You find my sister's murderer, and yes, that's what it is, not a laughing matter, not to mention my ma and grandma being raped. You're just as my ma said you would be." She turned and stormed away.

"Now hold on," he said, jumping to his feet. He raced past her and placed himself in front of the door. "Don't go away angry, please."

"Get out of my way."

"Alice, I'll look into this, and if I find something, I'll get some men together and ride out to look for these men, okay?"

"You need to go now," she growled.

Placing his hands on her shoulders, he squeezed and said, "If it will make you happy, me and my deputy will ride out this afternoon, alright?"

Cringing from his touch, she said, "Thank you. Now if you'll excuse me, I have to go bury my sister."

He frowned and stepped out of her way.

She threw open the door and left.

CHAPTER FIVE

JULY 11, 1895

TWO MILES SOUTH OF GREAT FALLS, MONTANA

Alice knelt down and scooped up a handful of the freshly dug earth and held it in her hand. She stared at it and remembered her and Martha working in the field just the other day. Her heart literally ached that now feet below her Martha lay wrapped in her favorite blanket and encased in a pine box. "I love you, Martha Mae."

Maggie and Anne stood behind Alice, both weeping.

"I'm gonna find those men, Ma, I'm gonna do it. If the sheriff won't, I will. If I do one thing in my life, it will be avenge my sister," Alice declared, tears streaming down her face.

Maggie stepped forward, placed her hand on Alice's shoulder, and squeezed. "You'll stay here. I won't lose both my daughters."

Alice clamped her hand closed, the moist dirt still in her palm. "But, Ma, someone has to do something."

"You're just upset, that's all," Maggie said. She wiped the tears on her cheeks with a handkerchief and walked away.

Alice watched her go inside the house. She glanced at Anne, who still stood solemnly, and asked, "Grandma, what do you think we should do?"

"Hon, you need to do what your ma says," Anne replied. "Now can you help walk me inside?"

Alice stood, dropped the clumped soil from her grasp, and offered Anne her arm.

Anne took it and pulled Alice close.

The two slowly walked across the uneven ground towards the house. Just before they reached the front porch steps, Anne stopped. "Alice, you're a very smart girl. In fact, if anyone has a future outside this town, it's you."

Alice stood and listened.

"I know I give many excuses for your ma's behavior since your pa died, but I have to admit now that I was wrong. Your ma has acted horribly towards you two girls, and there's no excuse for that. I pray you'll forgive me."

Alice scrunched her face, confused by the sudden apology. "Why are you now telling me this?"

"On account that poor little Martha is gone, I suggest you find your own way. I don't know what that is, but your ma will never recover from this. In fact, Martha's death will only make her life spin fully out of control. I don't want you here to see that."

"Are you telling me to leave?"

"I'm not telling you to pack your things and leave this very second. I'm suggesting that whatever plans you had for your life, they can include leaving this house and leaving this town," Anne explained.

Alice looked away, but her expression told Anne something.

"Were you already planning on leaving regardless of Martha?" Anne asked.

"I feel bad saying it, but yes," Alice confessed.

Patting her tenderly on the arm, Anne said, "It's fine, sweetheart, but I'm shocked that you would have left Martha here alone."

"It was something I've struggled with…" Alice said, tearing her gaze away from Anne to the grave site behind her. "I don't have to worry about that now."

"Where will you go? What will you do?"

"I don't know. I've thought about Seattle, even San Francisco."

"What will you do?"

"I haven't gotten that far in my plans. I figured I had time since I'm not eighteen yet," Alice said.

"But you'll be eighteen at the end of the month," Anne reminded her.

"I know, but what can an eighteen-year-old girl do in San Francisco?"

"She can do anything she sets her mind to."

"Not in this world, maybe one day a woman will have the same opportunities that men have, but I'm limited, you know this, Grandma," Alice lamented.

"And how were you planning on getting to San Francisco or Seattle?"

"I have some money from selling jams and jellies."

"That means you skimmed some money off the top. Weren't you supposed to give it all to your ma?" Anne asked with a devilish smile.

"Please don't tell," Alice pleaded.

"Girl, I won't say a word…about any of this. What I do ask is that you tell me what your plans are before you leave, can you do that?"

Cocking her head slightly and smiling, Alice replied, "I'll let you know."

"Very good, now please help me to my chair," Anne said, nodding towards the rocker on the porch.

"Grandma?"

"Yes, dear."

"All this talk about me leaving makes me feel horrible that nothing will be done about what happened to you, Ma and Martha," Alice said.

"What did you say about hoping that one day women will be given the same opportunities?"

"So we do nothing?" Alice asked.

"My dear, what can a girl do against those men? Are you going to ride out and find them? And what happens when you do? Are you going to gun them down, arrest them?"

"But something needs to be done," Alice urged.

"I couldn't agree more, but unless we hire a bounty hunter, or some man who's willing to help us strolls in here, which I doubt, we don't have a choice but to pray the sheriff will do his job."

"I despise this world," Alice seethed.

"It's cruel, harsh and unfair, but it's the only world we have. Now please, my bones are aching; help me to my chair."

Alice escorted her up the stairs and into the chair. "Grandma, I love you."

Patting Alice's hand, Anne said, "I love you too. Now can you—"

"Alice, come here!" Maggie hollered from upstairs.

Anne and Alice looked at each other, with Anne giving her a grimace. "You'd best go see what your ma wants."

"You know what she wants," Alice said, then sauntered inside the house.

GREAT FALLS, MONTANA

Harry and Henry exited the telegraph office to find Gus and Joseph missing. "Damn it, I told them to wait."

Henry looked down the street and saw where he thought they might have gone. "My money is on them being there."

Harry looked in the direction Henry was pointing, and saw a sign that read *SALOON*. "We don't have time for this, especially after what I just read."

"What did it say?" Henry asked.

Harry handed him the telegram along with the cypher he used to decode any messages, and strutted off towards the saloon. He burst through the swinging doors and glanced around once his eyes adjusted to the dim light.

Standing at the bar with a bottle of whiskey in front of them were Gus and Joseph.

Harry walked over and said, "I said you should wait."

"We are waiting," Joseph said before tossing back a shot. "And let me remind you that we've been waiting on word from the boss for two days now. So much for a telegram would be here for us."

"Joe is right. We've been camped outside town waiting for about two days now. So, any word?" Gus asked.

Henry entered, bellied up to the bar next to Gus, and grabbed the bottle. Not waiting for a glass, he tipped it back and chugged.

Harry gave Henry a displeased look and replied to Gus, "We're to set up an ambush."

"An ambush?" Gus asked. "What does that mean?"

"An ambush is—" Harry explained before being interrupted by Joseph.

"It means that Al was arrested and is being escorted to the border, that's what that means," Joseph said.

"He's been arrested?" Gus asked, wiping his mouth with his shirtsleeve.

"Marshals caught up with him outside Missoula. He's now being taken to the authorities near the border," Harry said.

"Told you," Joseph said.

"So we're gonna gun down some US Marshals?" Gus asked.

"It said to remove any threats, so yes, that's what we're being asked to do," Harry said, an uneasy feeling coming over him. He took the bottle away from Henry and took a drink.

Shocked to see Harry drink, Gus asked, "You feeling

alright?"

"No, I'm not. I didn't sign up for this job to go and kill marshals, or anyone, to be more specific. I'm not a killer," Harry answered.

"Son, don't you know who we're riding to go get?" Joseph asked.

Gus grinned, snatched the bottle from Harry's hands, and took a swig.

"I don't know who he is, I suppose," Harry said.

Joseph opened his mouth but stopped short of answering the question.

"Well, who is he?" Harry asked, with Henry and Gus looking on.

"He's an important man," Joseph said.

"Of course he must be, but who is he?" Harry asked.

"I don't know who he is, but if they're going through all this trouble to get him back, he must be," Joseph said.

"You don't know who he is?" Harry asked, confused.

"Not specifically," Joseph lied.

Grabbing the bottle back from Gus, Harry took another swig. He wiped his mouth and said, "I don't feel comfortable killing marshals. What do you fellas think about this?"

"I couldn't care less," Joseph said.

"Me either," Gus said.

"If they pay me more, then I'll do it," Henry said.

"We should renegotiate our payment. If we're being asked to kill lawmen, we need more money," Joseph said.

"They did offer that," Harry said to Henry. "Didn't you read the telegram?"

Looking down sheepishly, Henry replied, "I don't know how to read."

"Then why did you take the wire from me?" Harry asked.

"I asked you what it said; I didn't ask to read it," Henry shot back.

"Do you still have it?" Harry asked Henry.

Henry produced the folded paper from his pocket and set it on the bar.

Joseph grabbed it and unfolded it. His eyes scanned the few words written. "It doesn't say anything, just a bunch of jumbled letters."

"And the cypher?" Harry asked Henry.

"Oh yeah," Henry said, fishing around in his pocket. He removed the other paper and handed it to Joseph.

"How the hell do you use this?" Joseph asked, looking confused at both papers.

Harry rolled his eyes and said, "I don't have time to educate you on this, but trust me, it says that Al was arrested, he's being escorted along the northeast trail, and we're to set up an ambush immediately. The telegram is dated a day ago; this means they'll be riding through here by tomorrow, I suppose. They've offered us an additional one hundred each."

Looking confused, Joseph gawked at the paper and asked, "You got all of that from this?"

"Yes," Harry said, snatching both papers from Joseph. He folded them back up and stuffed them in his pocket. "I don't like this, not one bit."

"Well, it is what it is," Joseph said.

Taking the bottle into his grip, Harry poured a large amount into his mouth and swallowed. He set it back on the wet bar, gave each one a look, and said, "This is where I bid my farewell."

"You're leaving?" Joseph asked.

"I can't be part of this anymore. I was given bad information about the job. I can't be a party to murder," Harry said. He nodded to each one, turned, and headed for the exit.

The other three watched him leave, with Joseph getting to his feet.

"Where ya going?" Gus asked.

"I think you know," Joseph said.

"Oh," Gus said.

Joseph started for the door.

"Where's he going?" Henry asked.

"He's going to talk to Harry privately," Gus said. Turning back to the bar, he looked at the mostly empty bottle and cried out to the bartender, "Give us another bottle."

***

Harry signed the guest register and gave the clerk a smile.

The clerk handed him a key and said, "Room seven, top of the stairs, second door on the right."

"Thank you," Harry said. He picked up his saddlebag and sauntered slowly up the creaking stairs. He found his room, unlocked the door, and entered the tiny room. The first thing that hit him was the musty smell. He immediately opened a window and tossed his saddlebag on a chair. He plopped down on the bed and removed his hat. Looking at the inside rim of his hat, he didn't just see sweat stains but countless hours of work now gone and for nothing. He was deep inside Montana and had nothing to show for it. He thought about how he'd explain his returning home empty-handed to his wife and came to the conclusion that the best way to break the news was to be honest. She was like him and led a righteous life, so she'd understand. What he couldn't get past was what he'd do next. He needed money, and now he was unemployed once more with no new prospects on the horizon.

Tired from the long ride, he removed his boots and rubbed his sore feet.

In the corner of the room he spotted a tin plunge tub. The idea of having a bath sounded pleasing. All he needed to do now was make it happen.

After an hour of waiting, the last of the buckets of hot water were delivered. When the door closed, leaving him alone in the room, he gawked at the steaming tub. Not wanting to waste another second, he stripped down. Slowly he submerged himself into the water. The heat felt good and soothed his aching muscles. Using a towel as a pillow, he rested his head against it and closed his eyes; not a minute later he dozed off.

"Wake up," Joseph barked.

Harry opened his eyes, blinked repeatedly, and asked, "What the hell are you doing in my room?"

Sitting on the edge of the bed, with his pistol firmly

in his grip, Joseph replied, "I've come because you're not riding with us anymore."

Sitting up, Harry barked angrily, "I'm not going and that's that."

"You see, Harry, that's a problem."

Spotting the pistol finally, Harry asked, "What are you going to do, shoot me?"

Looking at the pistol, Joseph chuckled and said, "I thought about doing that at first, but I've changed my mind." He holstered the pistol and continued, "Harry, I don't know you, and I'll be honest, I never cared to."

"The feeling is mutual."

"I'm really an easygoing fella. I don't care what another man does as long as it doesn't interfere with what I'm doing."

"Listen, Joe, what is it you want?"

"I have a dilemma, and I'm vexed about how to proceed," Joseph said.

"I don't care about your dilemma. Now leave my room," Harry ordered.

"You see, Harry, I can't leave because you're the dilemma. I came here to shoot you, then I thought that doing so would cause too much attention, and I don't want that. So I'm sitting here thinking just how to handle this."

Unsure of how to act now that he'd been threatened, Harry was careful about how he spoke. "You're a smart man, Joseph. I saw that the first time we met. You have to understand that, as a family man, I can't participate in this any longer. Feel free to take my share of the job and just leave me be."

"I do plan on taking your share, but I'm not leaving here with you alive."

Sensing that Joseph wasn't lying, Harry grew tenser. His eyes darted around the room, looking for his pistol, only to see it on the chair in its holster and feet away from easily grabbing it.

"I'm a thorough man and planned everything out except how I'd do it, until I came up here. I suppose I thought that I'd have to get quite the jump on you, but now that I've found you naked and in the tub soaking, there's no need to cause such a ruckus."

"You've planned on murdering me since I left the saloon?" Harry asked.

"I did the very second you walked away. When you made your decision, you set your fate. I can't have someone all high and mighty running around, possibly talking to people about this job. Nope, that can't happen. The second you decided to leave, you made yourself a liability."

Raising his hands defensively, Harry pleaded, "I'm not going to say a thing. I just want to go home to my wife."

"Harry, that's just not going to happen. I'm sorry," Joseph said even though he wasn't really sorry.

"What can I do? Tell me, what can I say so you'll believe me?"

"There's nothing you can say, but what you can do is just go peacefully, don't make it difficult. I promise I'll make it painless."

Knowing now that Joseph was intent on killing him, Harry had only one choice, and that was to fight back. He leapt for his gun belt but came up inches short. Falling to the floor, he scrambled like a fish out of water, his wet feet and hands unable to get a grip.

Joseph jumped onto Harry's back, wrapped his right arm around his throat, and pulled back hard.

Harry lashed out as best he could, but Joseph had him in a naked rear choke hold.

Joseph squeezed as tight as he could while pulling back harder until he heard Harry's neck snap.

Harry's body went limp.

Feeling comfortable that he was dead, Joseph pulled the sheet from the bed and rolled Harry's body onto it, wrapping him up. He walked to the door, opened it and said, "Take him away."

Henry and Gus came into the room.

"What a dumb bastard." Gus chuckled.

"I kinda liked him. We had some good conversations," Henry said.

"Take him to the pig farm. I have it all arranged. When you're done, you can find me at the saloon," Joseph said.

Gus and Henry hauled away Harry's body.

While Harry had been preparing for his bath, Joseph had prepared for his death. He had followed him to the hotel and paid the clerk for information about Harry's room and where he could find a place to get rid of the body. Using pigs to devour a corpse was always a foolproof method, so he'd made those arrangements, then came back to find Harry at his most vulnerable in the bath. It was a good plan and, like so few, had worked out perfectly. Joseph wasn't lying to Harry about him being a liability. No one likes loose ends, and Harry had made himself one without consciously knowing he was. The thing was, Harry wasn't built for this type of work, and in the end, it cost him his life.

Joseph gathered up Harry's possessions, stuffed them in his saddlebags, and slung it over his shoulder. Just before he closed the door, he glanced at the tub and said, "A bath does sound good."

TWELVE MILES SOUTHWEST OF GREAT FALLS, MONTANA

Billy tied Al's horse to a tree and helped him out of the saddle. "Go over there and sit down. Don't even think about making a run for it."

Al gave Billy a glance and did as he said without muttering a muffled word, as the gag was still in his mouth.

After making their campsite for the night, Billy walked over to Hemsworth and sat down. "Can we talk?"

Biting into his hardtack, Hemsworth replied, "I'm all ears."

"About yesterday, I again overreacted and I'd like to apologize."

"There's nothing to apologize for, my friend. I was the one who stepped out of bounds."

"And you are a friend, you've been one since the first

day we met," Billy said.

"That's a nice thing to say," Hemsworth said as he chewed.

"And since you're my friend, I think I owe you a full explanation."

"No need. How about we just sit in silence and listen to the coyotes in the distance serenading us?" Hemsworth quipped.

Looking off towards the darkening sky, Billy said, "I suppose you must think me odd for not wanting to bed any woman who comes along."

"I wouldn't say you're odd; you're just not like many men who think with that thing between their legs. You have a code, a value system that men long for but are unable to keep. You're a true man of integrity. Though you have a temper now and then, you never truly waver, and I think that makes you an honorable man," Hemsworth said truthfully.

"You mean that?"

"I do, and I sensed that the first time we met, and you've only proven it over these past years. I have a lot to learn from you."

"Now that can't be true," Billy said, almost blushing from all the compliments.

"It is true. Few men stick to their values like you do. You're looking for a woman to have a life with, one you can trust to raise your children and instill those same values in them. I appreciate that and won't ever put you in a situation that challenges that."

"I want what my ma had. Their marriage was special,

a real love affair, but unfortunately he was taken too early."

"When I die, promise me you'll give the eulogy," Hemsworth said.

"Don't talk like that."

"I like to plan, sorry."

"You're not going anywhere anytime soon," Billy said.

Looking across the flickering flames of the campfire, Hemsworth said to Al, "It's day two and we're still alive. Looks like I win the wager."

Al mumbled something unintelligible then looked away.

"I'm serious, when I die, I want you to say great things about me," Hemsworth said as he snapped off a piece of the hardtack with his teeth.

"That'll be easy to do, so yes, I'll do it," Billy said. "And if I die, will you do the same for me?"

"It would be my honor, friend," Hemsworth said, adjusting his seating position. "My back is killing me. My body is taking a beating from all these years of riding."

"It's not the rides but the years; you're an old man," Billy joked.

"Ain't that the truth. Listen, I need to tell you something."

Seeing Hemsworth's expression changed, Billy asked, "What?"

"I think this may be my last ride," Hemsworth confessed.

"No."

"Yes, I am getting old, and to be honest, these jobs are wearing me out. I might have an opportunity at a desk job back in Coeur d'Alene."

"No, you can't go from riding a horse to riding a desk," Billy said.

"I didn't want to say anything until this was over, but I think I may have to hang up the old spurs."

Billy hung his head low and thought about the news. He then glanced over at Hemsworth with a supportive smile. "I'm happy for you. I hope it works out and you're able to get that position."

"It's not done yet, but before we left for Montana, I was given hope that it might happen."

"I suppose everything must come to an end at some point."

Chuckling, Hemsworth joked, "I haven't told my wife yet of the possibility. I'm afraid she'll not like the news."

"Just know that you'll always be welcome to come back anytime you want."

Al clapped then pretended to wipe a tear from his cheek.

"I do believe he's mocking us," Hemsworth said.

"I think you're right," Billy said.

"Remove his gag and give him this. We can at least provide him food and water."

Billy took a piece of hardtack and a canteen over to Al. He removed his gag and said, "Don't run your mouth if you know what's good for ya."

Famished and thirsty, Al grabbed the canteen with

his bound hands, pulled the cork out, and put it to his mouth. He guzzled the water, much of it running out from the sides of his mouth. He emptied it, burped, then took the tack and bit off a large chunk. With his mouth full, he said, "This stuff normally tastes like hardened horse dung, but when you're starvin', it tastes like the best thing I've ever eaten."

"You owe me for the wager," Hemsworth taunted.

"I'll pay you later, how does that sound?" Al sneered as he bit off another large chunk of the tack.

"Somehow I don't think you're one anyone can trust to pay their debts," Hemsworth said.

CHAPTER SIX

JULY 12, 1895

SEVEN MILES SOUTHWEST OF GREAT FALLS, MONTANA

"I still can't get rid of the image of those hogs just devouring poor Harry," Henry said.

"You keep saying poor Harry this, poor Harry that," Joseph sniped. "If you want to join your poor ole friend, just let me or Gus know and we can arrange it."

"I was just sayin'," Henry said.

"Well, stop saying it," Joseph said.

"Say, where should we set up this ambush?" Gus asked. He was sore, tired, and all he could think about was sleeping, having not slept much the night before.

"Just up ahead, I recall a nice rock outcropping off the road. There we'll have a good vantage point."

"Ah, this might sound like an odd question, but how will we know if they ride past?" Henry asked.

"We'll figure it out. Stop worrying about every little detail; you're starting to sound like your ole pal Harry," Joseph groaned.

The sound of horses and men talking came from just ahead.

Joseph raised his hand and said, "Shush, I hear something."

The three came to a stop and listened.

Joseph cocked his head and listened intently. The sounds of horses and chatter grew louder, meaning whoever it was were closer.

"Off the road," Joseph said, pointing to a grove of aspens nearby.

They turned their horses around, but it was too late. Over a small rise came the source of the sound; it was Hemsworth, Billy and Al.

Realizing they'd been spotted, Joseph said, "Come back around and head towards them; otherwise it will seem odd."

Gus and Henry did as Joseph said without complaint.

Joseph looked intently at the men and saw that the person in the saddle at the end was Al, the man they had been sent to rescue. "Well, I'll be damned, it's him," Joseph said.

"You sure? How do you know?" Henry asked.

"Al is the man riding on the last horse, with the gag in his mouth," Joseph informed the other two.

"What do we do?" Gus asked.

"We stand our ground and have them approach. We have them outgunned. We offer some conversation to lull them into thinking we're innocent travelers, then blast them. And, fellas, don't shoot Al."

"Which one is Al?" Henry asked.

"The one in shackles…damn fool," Joseph said.

***

"Riders ahead," Billy said.

"I see them," Hemsworth acknowledged.

"Should we ride around them?"

"No, keep going, but we should identify ourselves as marshals."

"You sure about this? Something doesn't feel right," Billy said.

"Is your gut telling you this, or do you see something not right?"

"My gut."

Hemsworth pulled back on the reins of his horse and came to a stop. Billy did the same. Holding up his hand, he hollered, "United States Marshals."

Joseph, Gus and Henry slowly rode up, stopping ten or so feet from Hemsworth.

"United States Marshals? How do I know you are who you say you are?" Joseph asked, leaning forward in his saddle, his right hand drawn back and casually sitting on his thigh.

Hemsworth pulled his overcoat to the side to show his badge.

Feigning that he couldn't see, Joseph squinted and said, "I see a badge that looks like a five-pointed star. Is that what marshals wear?"

"Let us pass. We have important business," Hemsworth said.

As Hemsworth talked, Billy eyed the three, paying close attention to where their hands were.

Joseph looked up to the late morning sky and said, "It's gonna be a hot one, I fear, scorching heat."

"Pull aside and let us pass," Hemsworth said.

"Marshal, the road is wide enough for both of us, can't you see?" Joseph said.

Hemsworth didn't reply. Like Billy, he sized the men up and could see they weren't normal travelers. By the way they were dressed along with how their gun belts were set up, these men just looked like trouble. "You're right, the road is wide enough. We'll be on our way."

"What did your prisoner do?" Joseph asked.

"He's a murderer, liar and cheat," Billy snapped.

"Sounds like he's a very bad man," Joseph said.

"He is," Hemsworth said.

"Where you taking him?" Joseph asked.

"You have a lot of questions for a passerby," Hemsworth said.

Henry was growing increasingly nervous. He knew that soon a fight would break out. He wasn't as skilled as Joseph or Gus, so to make sure he had somewhat of an edge, he slowly pulled his hand back near the grip of his pistol.

Spotting Henry's subtle movement, Billy barked, "You touch the grip of your pistol and I'll drop you."

Henry froze.

Joseph grinned and said, "Marshal, there's no need to threaten my man. He's just nervous is all."

"Why would he be nervous?" Hemsworth asked.

"Oh, he's not used to being around lawmen like yourself," Joseph replied.

"Or is it because he's a wanted man?" Billy asked.

A swift breeze swept over them and kicked up a dirt devil that whizzed around for a moment before dying out as quickly as it had formed.

The tension was building between the two groups, with neither wanting to initiate what they all knew was coming.

Hemsworth knew the advantage of winning any gunfight went to the man who drew first. So if there was to be a fight, he might as well draw first. The only issue was his right hand was on the horn of his saddle, a good foot and a half away from his Colt, which sat nestled in its holster.

Sweat beaded on Henry's brow and his hands began to tremble.

Billy kept his gaze upon Henry and his anxious behavior while also giving heed to the other two. Like Hemsworth, Billy knew whoever drew first was normally the winner in a gunfight.

Of them all, Gus sat silent in his saddle, his hand close to drawing his pistol.

Al could also sense that a fight was close to occurring, and if he had any chance of escaping, it would be now. With Billy and Hemsworth focused on the three, he decided he needed to create a distraction. He kicked his horse hard in the ribs; the jolt sent the horse rearing up enough to throw him.

Billy and Hemsworth both glanced back to see the commotion.

With Al's diversion, Joseph saw his opportunity. He

drew, cocked his pistol and fired. His first round missed Hemsworth by less than an inch.

Hemsworth not only heard the round crack but swore he also heard it whiz by his head. He and his horse spun around. He reached for his pistol, but before he could break leather, Gus had managed to get a shot off. This time the round hit Hemsworth in the left shoulder. He flinched from the blast but was able to rip his pistol from the holster. He cocked it, aimed and squeezed the trigger, his round striking Gus in the stomach.

Henry had his pistol out, cocked, and was aiming, but never managed to get a round off, as Billy had also drawn but fired his before. The .45-caliber round deeply grazed his head, ripping a piece of his scalp off, and sent him toppling off the horse, unconscious.

Joseph now had his pistol cocked again. He took aim on Hemsworth and fired. This time he didn't miss.

Hemsworth felt the bullet travel through him and exit. It was an odd sensation; he felt the searing pain followed by the gush of warmth as his blood poured from the wound. He looked down and saw the bloody hole in his vest and the blood beginning to soak through.

Seeing he'd hit Hemsworth with a potentially fatal shot, Joseph put his attention on Billy, only to see the muzzle of Billy's pistol trained on him. He ducked instinctually and in time to avoid being hit by Billy's second shot, which flew by and hit Gus.

Gus coughed and began to spit up blood. He clenched the wound in his neck, but seconds later he lost consciousness from blood loss and fell out of the saddle and onto the ground.

Al watched in horror as Gus fell. The fight was now between Joseph and Billy, as Hemsworth seemed unresponsive, slumped over in the saddle. Al ran towards Billy and kicked his horse.

Billy's horse reared, almost throwing him off.

This gave Joseph the time he needed. He cocked his pistol, took careful aim, and fired.

Billy groaned as the .45-caliber round slammed into his side. It traveled through the fleshy part of his lower abdomen and exited.

Al again went to kick Billy's horse, but this time Billy saw him coming. He cocked his pistol, and although he bent over in pain, he managed to get a shot off, striking Al in the gut.

Al dropped to his knees and fell over, reeling in pain.

Joseph cocked his pistol, aimed and fired, but once more missed. He cocked the pistol and fired again; this shot hit Billy in the upper part of his left shoulder.

Billy grunted in pain, swung around with his pistol, and went to shoot, but when he pulled the trigger, he found the chamber empty. Fear gripped him. He didn't have a second pistol, reloading would take too long, and going for his rifle in the scabbard wasn't practical with Joseph feet from him and his thumb pulling back his hammer again. He needed to flee and now. "Ya!" Billy shouted as he kicked the sides of his horse hard. The horse responded and took off.

Joseph aimed and pulled the trigger. But when the smoke cleared, he didn't see Billy fall. "How the hell did I miss again?" He watched Billy disappear over the rise.

When the dust settled, Joseph took a deep breath. He was amazed to have survived the ordeal without a scratch. Around him was carnage. He looked back and saw Gus and Henry down and not moving. He presumed them dead, but Al wasn't. He squirmed on the ground, crying in pain. Joseph dismounted and went to Al. "How bad is it?"

Al moaned, "It stings."

Joseph attempted to shift Al to get a better look but couldn't. "Would you stop moving? I'm trying to see how bad it is."

"It hurts real bad," Al whined.

Finally getting his shirt pulled up, Joseph could see the entry wound in his lower abdomen. He rolled Al onto his side and examined his back. "Clean through. Lucky bastard."

"You came for me."

Sweat beaded on Joseph's brow. "Of course I did."

Al and Joseph were friends from childhood but hadn't seen each other in over a decade. They both come to the States and become outlaws, with Al getting into fraud and gambling and Joseph becoming known as a hired killer, hence his nickname. Upon hearing through similar contacts that Al was on the run in Montana and needed some help, Joseph made himself available.

"Am I going to die?" Al asked.

"We need to get you mended up, but first we gotta get off this road," Joseph said, taking Al by the hand and helping him to his feet.

"Where?"

"I don't know, but we can't stay here."

"Wait, the fellas who were with you, are they dead?" Al asked.

"Everyone is dead, and if we don't get moving, we'll be dead too," Joseph said. "Can you ride?"

"Yeah," Al said. "But can you take these off?" he asked, showing Joseph his hands.

Joseph pulled the pin and removed the shackles. "Damn barbarians," he scoffed. He tossed the shackles onto the dusty ground.

Once both men were in the saddle, Joseph looked in both directions and said, "I recall seeing a cabin just up a ways. We'll go there."

"Shouldn't we get as far away as possible?"

"They'll think that. We'll hide right underneath their noses, and they won't even know it," Joseph bragged.

TWO MILES SOUTH OF GREAT FALLS, MONTANA

It took Billy a while to get his horse under control, and when he finally did, the blood loss was bringing on a state of vertigo. Seeing his blood-soaked shirt, he knew that the amount of blood he'd lost would soon lead to unconsciousness. He was in need of medical attention and quickly because what followed unconsciousness would be death.

He forced himself to sit tall in the saddle and scanned the area. In the distance he spotted a lone farmhouse with a single barn. "Let's go, boy," he said, nudging the horse forward.

He slowly trotted down the driveway.

The door of the house flew open, and out stepped Maggie with her shotgun in her hands. "Stop right there!"

"Please, I'm a United States Marshal and in need of help," Billy urged.

"I don't give a damn who you say you are. Just hold it right there," Maggie barked.

Billy raised a blood-covered hand and said, "Ma'am, I've been shot. I'm badly hurt and fear death may soon find me if I'm not attended to right away." He gasped after his long statement and lowered his weary head.

"Just turn your damn horse around and find somewhere else to go," Maggie hollered.

From her bedroom window, Alice watched. She noticed Billy seemed genuinely hurt, but after what had happened just days before, she didn't trust it.

Anne stepped out of the house and gave Billy a careful glance. "What's your name, son?"

"Don't talk to him like that, Ma," Maggie seethed.

"The boy looks hurt," Anne replied.

"My name is William Connolly, ma'am; I'm a deputy marshal. Please help me, my partner and I were ambushed not far from here. I fear he's dead, and I'll soon be if I'm not seen to," Billy said. He again gasped from the long reply.

"Where are you from, William Connolly?" Anne asked.

"Idaho, ma'am."

"Whereabouts in Idaho?"

"Why all the questions, Ma?" Maggie asked, the double barrels leveled at Billy, who sat in his saddle, wavering back and forth.

"Wallace, ma'am," Billy answered.

"What are you doing in Montana?" Anne asked.

"Damn it, Ma, stop asking him questions. He needs to go on about his business," Maggie said.

"The boy looks like he needs help, and if we can help him, we will. I know your animosity toward men, but we both know they're not all bad," Anne growled.

"Ma'am, I appreciate all the questions. I know you don't trust me, but I'm telling the truth. I've been shot twice, and my partner is probably dead. Please, I beg you, help," Billy pleaded.

"Answer the question," Anne insisted.

"We were escorting…" Billy said but stopped when he was overcome with an uncontrollable cough.

"Just get, go down the road a few miles. The Hamptons are a welcoming family; they'll give you aid," Maggie said.

"Ma'am, I don't think I—" Billy replied. He slouched forward and fell out of the saddle and onto the hard ground, followed by his horse collapsing from the wound it had received in the side.

"Damn!" Maggie shouted.

Anne slowly began to move towards Billy.

The door erupted open and out came Alice. She raced past Anne and towards Billy. Reaching him, she knelt and examined his wounds, to find he had been truthful. Turning back, she hollered, "He's hurt badly."

Shaking her head, Maggie groaned, "Fine, bring him inside."

"But I need help, Ma," Alice said.

"Damn fool woman," Maggie complained. She put her shotgun down and hurried to Alice. "I'll take his arms; you grab his legs."

"Okay, Ma," Alice said.

The two picked him up and carried him towards the house.

Anne opened the door, giving them a clear shot inside the house.

"Put him on the kitchen table," Maggie said.

"What about the couch?" Alice asked.

"I ain't about to have some stranger's blood soil and stain that couch. Your pa gave that to me," Maggie said.

"Just listen to your ma," Anne said.

They put Billy on the table.

Alice looked down at Billy's ashen face and said, "Will he die?"

"I don't know, but if you don't want him to, you'll need to do everything I ask," Maggie said.

"Yes, Ma," Alice said, nodding.

Maggie ran through a small list of items she needed.

Alice raced off to get them.

With Alice out of the room, Maggie leaned close to Billy and said, "Boy, if you're lyin', I'll kill you myself, you hear me?"

"I don't think he can," Anne said.

"You're my witness. If he does one thing, I'll end

him," Maggie said.

"Just help the poor lad. You can see he's truly hurt," Anne said.

Blood began to pool on the table and drip off the edge.

Alice reappeared with the items minus one. "I need to get a pot of water boiling."

"Hurry up about it, then," Maggie said. She put her attention back on Billy, grabbed hold of his shirt, and tore it open. "Now let's see how bad you are."

SIX MILES SOUTHWEST OF GREAT FALLS, MONTANA

Joseph patched Al up as best he could and let him lie in front of a fire he'd made inside the small dirt-floor cabin. It didn't take Al but a minute to fall fast asleep.

With Al taken care of, Joseph sat down and sorted through a basket he'd found on a table in the cabin. His eyes widened with joy as he discovered jerky and a couple of apples. "My lucky day, I love apples. What about you?" he asked the young boy who sat opposite him, next to the front door, his legs pulled up close to his chest and a look of terror on his small chubby face. "You're a quiet one, huh?"

The boy remained silent, his eyes fixed on the deathly stares of his parents lying dead across the room in a pool of blood.

Joseph had arrived at the cabin, found it occupied, but that never stopped him. He quickly laid waste to the parents, but his code wouldn't allow him to harm children. He gave a glance over to the dead bodies and smirked. "It's bothering you, isn't it?"

The boy sat silent.

"Oh, alright," Joseph said, getting to his feet. He found a blanket folded in a trunk and tossed it over the bodies. "Does that help?"

Tears streamed down the boy's face. He was about six years old and had never experienced such brutality and savagery until Joseph made his appearance.

"Listen, boy, get a good cry out, then give it a rest. When I lay my head down to get some sleep, you'd best be done with your sniveling," Joseph said before taking a large bite of the apple. Juice glistened on his beard. "Where did your ma get these apples? They're damn good."

"Why?" the boy asked.

"Why what?" Joseph asked. He saw the boy was looking at the blanket and said, "Oh, that. Listen, you were going to grow up anyways and hate them. You see, it's natural for children to reach a certain age then hate their parents."

"Will you kill me?" the boy asked.

"Nah, I don't kill children, but if you give me any grief, I'm not opposed to disciplining you harshly. I've got a nice thick belt and don't mind using it. Are you going to be giving me any grief?"

The boy shook his head.

"Good," Joseph said. "What's your name?"

"Adam."

"Hmm, my name is Joseph, and don't think you can call me Joe. I'm not a fan of that."

"Was he shot?" the boy asked, pointing to Al.

"Yep, got shot in the gut," Joseph replied, taking his last bite. He tossed the apple core into the flames. "Tell me, Adam, do neighbors stop by here much?"

Adam shook his head.

"Anyone else I should be expecting? Best you tell me 'cause it will save their lives. If you lie and someone comes here, I'll end their lives like I did your parents'," Joseph threatened. "I'll ask you again, anyone coming around here?"

Adam shook his head and said, "No, sir."

Joseph looked around the single-room cabin. If one were to walk through the front door, they'd look left and see the fireplace against the wall. Directly in front of them sat a table; this not only served as the central location for the family to eat but literally served as the central location for anything that happened in the house. The only chairs in the cabin were around it, and they totaled five. Behind the table on the opposite wall was a small window, where a thin white sheet hung, no doubt used more for privacy than anything. This was where Joseph was sitting, just below the window, with a clear view of the door. To the right, a small cot, just big enough to barely hold two adults, was shoved in the corner. "Where do you sleep?" Joseph asked, noticing only the cot and no other bed.

Adam pointed to a corner near the fireplace. There, stacked up, was a small pillow and some folded clothes.

"You sleep there, next to where Al is lying?"

Adam nodded.

"Well, it's a good thing your parents didn't have any more children." Joseph chuckled. "If you want, you can go lie down." Joseph took a piece of jerky and bit off a large chunk. As he chewed, a bit got stuck in between two molars he'd been having trouble with. "Ouch," he bellowed. He rubbed his jaw and scowled. "I need to get that tooth yanked out." He caught sight of a book near the pillow where Adam said he slept and asked, "What's that book there?"

"*Moby-Dick*," Adam answered.

"You read? I managed to read myself. How about you read me a chapter or so?"

Adam shook his head.

"Go ahead, get the book and read to me," Joseph insisted.

"I don't want to," Adam said.

Joseph's demeanor grew stern and he growled, "Get the damn book, boy, and read."

Adam hopped up, scurried over, and took the book. He went back to his spot near the door and sat.

"Read whatever you like. I'm going to try to rest a bit," Joseph said, leaning back and tipping his hat to cover his eyes.

Adam opened the book and thumbed through the brittle pages. He stopped on a word he could read and said, "The." He paused and began to cry.

Hearing Adam's sobs, Joseph seethed, "Stop crying, boy, and read."

"The men," Adam said and again stopped to cry

loudly.

Lifting his hat, Joseph barked, "Boy, if you wake my friend, I'll give you a good beatin'."

Adam lowered the book and sobbed louder.

"Shut it," Joseph growled.

Heeding Joseph's order, Adam choked back his tears and mumbled, "Sorry." He wiped his face with his hands and sat staring down at the open book.

"Read," Joseph ordered.

"I can't," Adam whined.

"Why's that?"

"I'm scared."

"Boy, you have nothing to be afraid of; I don't kill children. You could say it's a code I live by, so you don't have to worry about that."

"But you said you'd hurt me," Adam said, sniffling.

"I will, but I won't kill ya. Just don't do anything that would lead to gettin' hurt and you'll be fine. Now, open the damn book and read me a chapter," Joseph barked.

Adam opened the book again and began to recite what words he did know, making the reading choppy.

Joseph sighed and said, "You don't know how to read, do ya?"

"No, sir."

"Then why do you have that book over near your things?"

Adam faced the open book towards Joseph and pointed at the sketch of Captain Ahab on the inside flap.

"Oh, I see, you look at the pictures," Joseph said.

"I can read some, but my..." Adam said before

pausing.

"Your what?"

"Do I have to read?"

"I suppose not, but I do need you to come here," Joseph said.

Adam lowered the book and gulped.

"Come here," Joseph ordered.

Adam shook his head and a look of terror spread across his face.

"I told you I'm not going to kill you, and I have no reason to hurt you. Now come here," Joseph said.

Putting the book on the floor, Adam slowly rose and timidly walked over to Joseph. He stopped just outside arm's length away and kept his head down.

"Closer," Joseph said.

Shuffling his feet, Adam moved closer.

When he could reach him, Joseph grabbed him forcibly and pulled him close. "I said come here."

"Please, no, don't hurt me," Adam pleaded.

"I'm not, I'm just gonna tie you up so you don't run off," Joseph said, taking some of the extra cloth bandages he had and using them to secure Adam's wrists and ankles together. He tied the last knot and said, "Now hop your ass back over there and sit down."

Adam did as Joseph said. As he lowered himself back down, a sense of relief filled him that he hadn't been hurt.

Joseph chuckled at how the boy was acting. He was sadistic in how he treated people and was taking joy from the fact he scared Adam. Feeling a heavy fatigue wash over him, he tipped his hat forward and leaned back against the wall. A few hours of sleep would be beneficial; then he'd think about his next move.

Adam sat still, his gaze fixed on Joseph. A shadow in the window above Joseph caught his attention. He stared until he spotted who he suspected it was: his brother, Clive.

Clive was four years older than Adam and had been out hunting when Joseph and Al arrived. He returned to see the horse, and instead of going into the cabin, he thought to peer into the window. What he didn't expect to see was Adam tied up and his parents lying dead on the floor.

CHAPTER SEVEN

JULY 13, 1895

TWO MILES SOUTH OF GREAT FALLS, MONTANA

The initial sounds Billy heard were voices. They were muted at first, but as he began to wake, they grew louder. He opened his eyes, but the bright light of the early morning hurt his eyes, forcing him to close them.

The voices stopped.

"Where am I?" Billy asked, his eyes still pressed closed.

"Are you Deputy US Marshal Connolly?" Amherst asked.

Billy tried to open his eyes again, this time doing so slowly. He blinked repeatedly until his vision became clear. He glanced at the unfamiliar faces and asked, "Where am I?"

"Son, answer my question. Are you—?"

"I am and who are you?" Billy asked.

"I'm the Cascade County sheriff," Amherst said.

"Sheriff, I'm glad to see you. I need your help," Billy said. He went to sit up but was stopped when a jolt of pain similar to an electric shock shot through his body.

He lay back down and said, "My partner, Marshal Hemsworth, I need to find him."

"Son, I have some bad news," Amherst said. "Your partner is dead."

The pain of hearing what he feared was true was worse than anything he'd ever dealt with since hearing his father had died. Tears wet his eyes, but he stopped short of crying. He wanted revenge, and if he were to get it, he'd have to remove any sort of emotion. "Have you found Al?"

"Who?" Amherst asked.

"Our prisoner, he goes by the name Two-faced Bob, but his real name is Alfred Cummins."

"I'm not sure. We found two other bodies, and one of them could be Two-faced Bob. When you're well enough, you should come to town. We have the bodies on ice. Can you describe the men who attacked you?"

Billy looked at Amherst and asked, "Can someone help prop me up?"

Standing in the back of the room were Maggie, Anne and Alice. Upon hearing Billy needed help, Alice sprang into action and came forward. She took a spare pillow, and as she helped lift him up, she shoved the pillow behind him. "There you go," she said.

Billy replied, "Thank you." He caught a good look at her and paused. He was instantly captivated by her beauty.

"Will there be anything else?" Alice asked.

Staring at her, he was lost in her blue eyes.

"Sir, anything else?" Alice asked.

"Ah, no, no, I'm fine. That was what I needed," he said, finding himself to be instantly nervous.

She gave him a pleasant smile, gently touched his shoulder, and said, "Please call on me if you need anything."

"I will," Billy said.

"Alice Marie, you get back over here," Maggie said in a scolding tone.

Alice gave Billy one more gleaming look and walked off.

"Deputy Marshal Connolly, can you please describe the men who attacked you and your partner?" Amherst asked.

"There were three of them," Billy said. "One was a very tall man, I could tell by how high he sat in the saddle. He had black hair and snarled when he talked. The other men were shorter, one was rounder in the waist, and the other, well, he seemed more timid, scared, you could say."

"I appreciate the description of their demeanor, but can you describe their appearance?" Amherst asked.

Billy pressed his eyes closed and thought. "I never saw them standing, only on horseback. I can only assume the others were shorter, but they appeared to be maybe shorter than six feet, but one man, the tall one, he was clearly well over six feet."

Alice recalled the man who had attacked her, Joseph, standing tall. "I think that's the man who attacked me."

"Alice, don't interrupt the sheriff," Maggie said.

Amherst glanced over his shoulder and said, "Alice,

now's not the time."

"How do you know those aren't the men? First we get attacked, now those marshals. Attacks like these aren't everyday events. I think they could be related."

"You were attacked?" Billy asked Alice.

"About three days before you arrived. Ma turned them away; they returned and—"

"That's enough," Maggie said.

"I'm sorry to hear it," Billy said. "I'm sure you told the sheriff here."

Alice cut Amherst a harsh look and replied, "I did."

"And you sent out a posse to look for these men, of course?" Billy asked.

"Well, I was investigating the merits of the case and was close to—"

"You didn't send men out to look for them?" Billy asked, shocked upon hearing the sheriff's incompetence.

"It's a long story, one I'll share with you when you come into town," Amherst replied.

"No, Sheriff, please enlighten the nice marshal now," Alice blurted out.

"Alice, watch your tongue," Maggie barked.

"No, I won't," Alice said. "Men attacked us and now Martha is dead."

"Who's Martha?" Billy asked.

"She's my sister and died from an injury inflicted on her that night," Alice answered.

Hearing the news of the girl's death, Billy scowled and said, "Sheriff, we can discuss this later, and I need this young woman here to help describe those men 'cause they could be the same."

"Did one of the men have a wound on his arm?" Alice blurted out.

"I'll ask the questions," Amherst snapped. He was growing agitated with Alice.

"A wound?" Billy asked.

"The tall man, he attacked me, and I managed to stab him with a knitting needle in his left forearm, right about here," Alice said, pointing at a spot on her forearm to illustrate.

Billy thought hard and remembered the tall man had his sleeves rolled up because it had been hot that late morning. He even recalled him talking about the heat. He pressed his eyes closed and tried to recall. He could see the man in the saddle, his snarled facial expression and jet-black hair that jutted out from underneath the brim. He recalled seeing his right arm pulled back and his left arm resting on the horn of the saddle. He thought hard about the left arm and..."Yes. He had a bandage on his left forearm."

"It's them. I knew it, I knew those men would do further harm!" Alice squealed with delight, knowing that she now had a chance to finally catch or at least begin pursuit of the men who were to blame for what had happened to her family. "And that man in question is Joseph Paul King."

Amherst's anger reached an apex. He turned towards Alice and hollered, "You damn little..." He bit his lip and continued, "How dare you stand here and embarrass me in front of the marshal? How dare you act pompous when your mother, your—"

"Sheriff, that's enough!" Billy snapped.

"Marshal, you need to know," Amherst replied to Billy.

"I don't need to know anything from you that I already haven't seen. You, sir, are not a cordial or polite man. You stand here and demean these women. They have suffered at the hands of the very men who killed my partner and wounded me, yet because of your incompetence, you didn't pursue. You, sir, don't deserve to wear the badge, because it represents the law, and the law is impartial in whom it serves."

Amherst's nostrils flared and his face flushed red. "I won't stand here and be berated by a harlot's daughter and a marshal who isn't older than my own son."

"Me or my age isn't the problem here, you are. You were even given a name yet did nothing?" Billy fired back.

With his fists clenched, Amherst screamed, "I won't stand here and suffer these indignities." He snatched his hat from the table near him and marched out of the bedroom.

Maggie glared at Alice then followed Amherst out. "Oh, Sheriff, please don't go."

Finding humor and justice in the exchange, Anne gave Alice and Billy a wink and said, "Bravo to you two. I've never liked that crusty old son of a bitch anyhow."

"Grandma, your language." Alice blushed.

Anne patted Alice's shoulder and said, "Good job, honey, good job." She slowly walked from the room and into the hall.

With only Alice and Billy left in the room, Billy grew nervous. He cleared his throat and said, "I've met other lawmen like him and I find them despicable. Much of what happened to me could have been averted had he done his job. I pray that no one else fell victim to those men."

"Thank you for defending me," Alice said as she fidgeted with a strand of hair that fell near her cheek.

"What he was doing to you was wrong. It's important for men to stand up for women. My father taught me that. I'm not saying women aren't capable, I'm merely stating that it's a man's duty to honor and revere women."

"I didn't take what you said as an insult, and I truly am grateful," Alice said. "Can I get you anything? Are you hungry or thirsty?"

"I could use a glass of water and my clothes."

"Your clothes?"

"Yes, if I'm going to hunt those men down, it would help if I'm dressed," Billy quipped.

"Your clothes were destroyed. My ma had them burned, but shouldn't you be resting?"

"No, I need to go looking for Al and the other men right away. I need to also get a telegram to Coeur d'Alene and tell them what's happened. I'll need some support."

"Are you sure?" she asked.

"I'm positive," Billy said. No matter how bad he'd been hurt. The longer he didn't do anything, the harder it would be to catch Al and the others.

"You look about the size of my pa. I'm sure you can use some of his."

"Thank you," Billy said, sitting up taller in the bed. He swung the sheet off him and went to swing his legs out of the bed, then realized awkwardly that she was standing there staring at him.

Alice watched then realized she was gawking at him. "I'm sorry, forgive me. I'll be right back," Alice said and sped for the door. She exited the room, closing the door behind her.

Alone, Billy looked around the room. Next to him was a small nightstand with an oil lamp in the center. On the wall nearest the door was a dresser. Sitting atop it was a stack of books, the spines facing away, making it difficult for Billy to read the titles. In the corner a child-sized rocking chair stood, a porcelain doll in the seat. He then realized that the room was probably Alice's sister's. He looked for his boots and gun belt but didn't see them. A desire burned in him to find the men responsible and slay them where they stood. He knew he still had a responsibility to find Al and bring him to the border, but right now his main concern was finding the men who had killed Hemsworth, and end their lives. He put his feet on the cool floor and stood. The pain in his side burned, but it wasn't as bad as the first time he felt the wound. He wasn't sure how bad his injuries were, but upon Alice's return, he'd find out.

Tapping at the door told him she was there. "Come in."

The door opened and in came not only Alice but

Maggie.

Maggie marched up to Billy, hands planted on her hips, and said firmly, "Those clothes were my husband's. I expect you to wear and appreciate them. Those trousers were his favorite."

"I will, ma'am," Billy said, almost wanting to laugh at Maggie's odd behavior. He inhaled and could smell whiskey.

"Alice here tells me you're going to go find those men," Maggie said.

"Yes, ma'am, right away," Billy said. "First I'm going to head into town, meet the sheriff, who I expect will give me a chilly reception, but nevertheless he'll be forced to help me. I will do my best to garner any clues from the dead man's belongings, and from there I'll ride out to where we were ambushed to see if I can find anything of value."

"Hmm, you seem like a smart man, thorough, I like it," Maggie said, sizing Billy up and down. She stepped forward, bent down and reached for him.

"What are you doing?" Billy asked, recoiling from her initial touch.

"Boy, I'm just checking your bandages. You do know you were damn lucky those bullets passed through you without causing any real damage."

Giving in, he allowed her to examine the bandages. He felt awkward as Alice watched intently from behind her mother, especially when his shirt was off.

"Still looks good. You know the doc was impressed with the work I did on you," Maggie said.

"Ma'am, thank you for taking care of me. I don't think I would've made it," Billy said.

"You need to thank my ma. She was the one who made this happen. If it were up to me, I would've sent you packing," Maggie said.

"Ma, don't say that," Alice said.

"You know it's true. I don't much like men, can't trust them," Maggie said.

"Well, ma'am, I can understand why after all you've been through," Billy said.

Finished, Maggie stood back up and said, "You look good, no infection, but you'll need to keep it clean."

"I'll do my best," Billy said.

"Alice, give him the clothes," Maggie ordered.

"Ma'am, where are my boots and gun belt?" Billy asked.

"In the trunk at the foot of the bed," Maggie answered, pointing to it.

He looked around the bed and saw it. "Good, thank you."

"And your horse, he died right where he fell, I'm sorry. It looked like a fine creature," Maggie said.

"Can I borrow a horse?" Billy asked, this time locking eyes with Alice.

Alice blushed and said, "Of course."

Seeing the two stare at each other, Maggie cleared her throat and said, "Alice, come, let's let the marshal get dressed."

"Yes, Ma," Alice said sheepishly, tearing her gaze away from Billy.

"This is a nice room. Was this your daughter's room?" Billy asked Maggie.

"It was," Alice answered instead.

A painful look hit Maggie. "My poor little dove, taken way too early." She lowered her head and took in a deep breath. "Marshal, promise me you'll find those men."

"I promise," Billy said.

"And promise me you'll put a bullet in them," Maggie said.

"I promise," Billy said.

"And one more thing, promise me before you kill them that they know," she said, pausing as she began to choke on her own words.

Alice went to her mother and embraced her.

"I'm fine, I'm fine," she said, wiping a tear from her cheek. "You let them know that their deaths are not payment enough for what they did; that they'll burn in the eternal fires of hell. Can you tell them that?"

Unsure if he could remember all she'd said but not one to tell a grieving mother no, he said, "I promise they'll know."

"Good, thank you," Maggie said. She wiped a couple more tears then hastily rushed out of the room. "Come, Alice."

"Coming, Ma," Alice said, waiting for Maggie to disappear. When she thought she was gone and out of earshot, Alice turned to Billy and whispered, "Take me with you."

"What?"

"Please take me with you. I want to help you. I want to be the one to avenge my sister," Alice said.

"No, that's not going to happen."

"Please," Alice begged.

"I can understand your anger, I really can, but you're a girl and those men, they're dangerous."

"I can help. I know this county like the back of my hand," she declared.

"Not going to happen. I'm grateful for everything you did, but you're not going to ride with me."

Distraught, she lowered her gaze and said, "Please, I can be of help."

"No, I'm a lawman, you're not; this is what I do. Again, I'm more than grateful for what you've done."

"I'll leave you to get dressed. I hope that you'll reconsider," Alice said, turned and left Billy alone in the room.

SIX MILES SOUTHWEST OF GREAT FALLS, MONTANA

Adam woke to find Joseph curled up on the floor, snoring. The dim light coming from the window above Joseph told him that it was morning. He glanced over to Al to see he had rolled onto his other side; it was evident that he was alive.

A shadow in the window above Joseph caught Adam's attention. He stared until he spotted who he suspected it was, his brother, Clive.

Clive was four years older than Adam and had been

out on a hunting trip. He had planned to return that morning and, like clockwork, here he was.

Adam had kept that information from Joseph. He was six but had been educated on the art of deception from his father, and knew that if he was to survive, his brother was his only chance.

Clive's suspicious and curious mind had him peek in the window versus just walking in the door upon seeing the strange horses hitched outside. When he caught sight of Adam tied up on the floor, he was shocked but was ready to help out his brother in any way he could.

Motioning with his head, Adam signaled for Clive not to enter.

The two brothers were close, and Clive picked up from Adam's head movements that he wanted him to go get help. Unsure if that was wise, he held up his rifle and pointed, signaling that he could come inside and start shooting.

Adam shook his head and mouthed the word *sheriff.*

Clive nodded, turned and sprinted towards town.

Joseph opened his eyes and looked at Adam. He noticed he was staring at the window and shot up. He craned his head back, pulled the drape to the side, and peered outside to see nothing but a small dirt lot and the trees beyond. "What were you looking at?"

"Nothing," Adam replied.

"Tell me, boy, was someone there?" Joseph said, getting to his feet.

"No, sir, I just woke is all," Adam lied.

Joseph turned back and said, "If you're lyin', I'll hurt

you, do you understand?"

Adam nodded.

Joseph stumbled over to Al and knelt down. He saw beads of sweat on his brow. He felt his forehead and said, "Damn, he's burning up."

"It's infected," Adam said. "My ma says that if you have a fever after getting a bad cut, you have an infection."

Joseph rolled Al onto his back.

Al grunted in pain and opened his eyes barely a slit. "I don't feel good."

"It's infected, that's why," Joseph said, peeling back the sticky bandages to reveal a swollen red wound.

"How did it get infected so fast?" Al asked.

Joseph stared at the wound. He didn't need to see the exit wound to know it probably looked equally as bad. He sighed as he pondered what to do. He wasn't knowledgeable about how to handle such things outside of just bandaging them up. "Boy, do you know how to treat wounds?"

Looking bewildered, Adam replied, "No, sir."

"Of course, I'm stupid; you're just a damn child," Joseph grunted.

Al pointed to the hot embers in the fire.

"You want me to cauterize it?" Joseph asked.

"Yes."

"Are you sure?"

"Yes," Al answered.

"Very well," Joseph said. He took the fire poker and placed it in the center of the simmering coals and waited.

After a few minutes he pulled it out and saw that it was red. He put it back in and unbuckled his belt. He folded it over and said, "Bite down on this." He placed the belt between Al's teeth and removed the fiery hot poker.

Al's eyes watched the poker as it glided towards the wound on his abdomen.

Joseph didn't waste time; he set it directly on top of the wound and pressed down.

Al groaned as he bit down on the belt, his eyes bulging.

"Almost done," Joseph said.

The smell of burning flesh rose, forcing Joseph to turn his head away.

Satisfied that he'd done enough, he put the poker back in the embers. He rolled Al onto his side and said, "I gotta do the back too."

The pain was excruciating, but Al was willing to suffer it if it helped.

After waiting another few minutes, he removed the searing hot poker and placed it on Al's skin. An audible sizzle could be heard.

Al's body tensed. He whimpered, as the pain was proving to be difficult to handle.

Feeling that he'd done what was necessary, Joseph pulled the poker off Al's skin; however, when he pulled it away from Al's skin, it took some of his flesh with it.

Al shrieked.

The scene before Adam was shocking. He'd never seen a wound cauterized.

Unfamiliar with how to handle wounds, Joseph

simply pulled the soiled bandage back up to cover the area. "All done."

Al spit out the belt. His breathing was elevated as if he'd just sprinted a hundred yards.

"That should do it…right?" Joseph said, unsure of what he'd just done, and he hoped it fixed the issue. "You just lie there, okay." Joseph crawled back to his spot under the window and gave Adam a smile. "That was something, wasn't it?"

Adam didn't reply. He simply stared at Joseph.

"Are you hungry?" Joseph asked.

Adam nodded.

Seeing the basket from the day before, Joseph pushed it towards Adam. Then he noticed Adam was still bound. "Ah, that's a problem." He got up and untied his arms. "Now eat."

Adam shifted through the basket and took out a piece of jerky. His stomach ached, but his appetite wasn't really there. The smell of the dried meat made him feel nauseous. Unable to eat, he put it back, lowered his head, and began to cry.

"What the hell you crying for?" Joseph asked.

"I want my ma," Adam moaned.

"Well, boy, that ain't gonna happen. Get over it," Joseph snapped.

"When will you let me go?" Adam asked.

Joseph leaned forward and said, "Not sure, hell, I might even take you with us."

Adam lifted his head and cried out, "No, please don't."

"Stop your crying and eat or I'll give you a real reason to cry," Joseph threatened.

Pressing his eyes closed, Adam prayed that Clive would come back soon and with help.

TWO MILES SOUTH OF GREAT FALLS, MONTANA

The stairwell railing creaked each time Billy put his weight on it. When he reached the ground level, he looked around and wondered where everyone was. "Hello?"

"Out front," Anne called.

Billy sauntered to the front door slowly and peeked outside to find Anne sitting in her rocker, smoking a pipe. "Good day, ma'am."

"You're looking better than when we first met," Anne said. She exhaled a large puff of smoke.

"On account of you, thank you," Billy said. "Say, I'm looking to borrow a horse. I need to—"

Alice appeared around the corner, walking a horse. "He's fed and I even brushed him."

"Thank you." Billy steadily walked down the porch steps and met her halfway. Taking the reins, he leaned close and whispered, "You've been most kind. I don't know how I'll ever pay you back."

Whispering back, Alice said, "You can take me with you."

"You're being foolish," he replied. "I've already told you I'm not taking you with me."

"I need to do this, I must," she said. "They killed my

sister and I mean to exact revenge on all of them."

"Why are you whispering over there?" Anne cried out, sitting in a cloud of smoke.

"We're not, Grandma, you're just deaf," Alice hollered back. "Now, let me go with you," she said, immediately putting her focus back on Billy.

Looking over his shoulder and back, Billy said, "Suppose I said yes. How am I to explain taking you with me? Just tell me how I'm supposed to make that happen."

"I'll leave a note upstairs, which my ma will find later."

"Not to your ma, although that's a tricky situation to say the least. How am I going to explain to the people I answer to back in Idaho?"

"Don't tell them," Alice said.

"This is foolish," Billy said. He removed his hat and wiped his brow. "Darn, it's already so hot."

"Welcome to summer in Montana," she quipped.

"Why is it that everyone here is a pain? Can you explain that? First the sheriff—I never thought to ask, but I'm willing to wager he hasn't sent men out to track Al, and now I have you, a pretty little thing with a sharp tongue and a gentle heart determined to get me into trouble and talking about revenge."

"You think I'm pretty?"

Embarrassed, he answered, "Oh, I meant…"

"It's okay, I hear it a lot," she teased.

"I meant no disrespect," he said, his tone showing how awkward he felt.

"And I have a sharp tongue?"

"I meant that you look like this and, well, you helped save me, but you stand there talking about avenging your sister, which can only mean killing them."

"Men who killed my sister and raped my ma and grandma!" she barked. This time her voice rose above a whisper.

"What are you kids talking about over there?" Anne asked.

"Just about what happened is all, Grandma," Alice replied and continued with Billy. "Do you want to find this Al person?"

Grinding his teeth, Billy said, "I'm going into town. If I need your help, I'll ask." He climbed atop his horse and gave her a quick glance. "Please don't misconstrue that I'm not grateful; I just can't be taking a young girl with me."

"Young girl? I'm old enough to handle myself," Alice snapped.

"How old are you?"

"Seventeen, but I'll be eighteen soon, and I mean soon."

"Does your mother or grandmother know you're asking to ride with me?" Billy asked.

"Of course not, and if they found out, I couldn't care less, so you can't use that against me," she replied.

Maggie emerged from the house, holding an empty whiskey bottle. Spotting Alice, she said, "There you are."

Seeing her mother put a rare smile on Alice's face. She cut her eyes at Billy and said, "You'd best wait up."

"I need you to run into town for some supplies,"

Maggie said.

"I can do that, Ma," Alice said.

Billy shook his head, as he knew what was coming next.

Alice jogged over to Maggie and said, "The marshal should escort me on account of what happened."

Maggie scrunched her face. She didn't like the idea, but she couldn't fathom living another hour without her booze. "Fine, but you stay an arm's length away from him at all times, and take this." She pulled out the pistol she'd let her borrow before and handed it to her.

Alice took the pistol and shoved it into a pocket. "I'll be fine. I don't think he's like most men."

"Don't be fooled. Behind the handsome mug could lie a scoundrel," Maggie said sternly. "Mr. Marshal, would you please escort my only living daughter into town and back?" she asked, stressing the *only living daughter* part of her question.

Billy grunted. How could he say no? These were the people who had saved him, and he was going that way anyway. To say no would be impolite. "Yes, ma'am. It would be my honor."

Alice walked over to him, a skip in each step, and said, "Wait right here. Let me saddle up a horse."

GREAT FALLS, MONTANA

The ride into town wasn't a pleasant one for Billy. Both his side and shoulder hurt badly, but listening to Alice tell stories of her life and youth did help ease the pain. For someone only seventeen, she seemed very mature, yet he could still hear the youthfulness in the way she described certain things. It was the sort of optimism you'd expect from someone her age. He recalled having it as well. They had something in common: both had lost their father, and both had dealt with the rape of their mother. Coincidentally he had been seventeen too when his mother had been raped. He understood her desire to seek revenge; hell, he'd actually gone and killed the men personally. Yet here he was telling her she had no right to do what he felt came naturally. Maybe he was wrong in denying her the chance, he thought. After all, his actions had led to him meeting Hemsworth and eventually to becoming a marshal.

She guided him through Great Falls until they reached the sheriff's office. Through the windows of the office, he could see Amherst. He was talking and moving his arms wildly. Was he talking to one of his deputies about the treatment he'd encountered back at the house? Was he about to walk into a hornet's nest?

"This is where I leave you, for now," Alice said. "I'm going just down the street. It will only take me ten minutes at most."

Knowing he had to escort her back, he said, "I will be longer. Is there somewhere else you can go while I do what I need to do?"

"No."

He thought for a second and said, "Then wait for me out here."

"I can do that," she said and moved on down the

street.

He watched her trot off, not out of a sense of duty but because he wanted to watch her go.

The door to the sheriff's office opened, and heavy footfalls sounded, pulling Billy's attention away from Alice.

"Do United States Marshals babysit now?" Amherst mocked.

Next to Amherst stood another man, a badge on his chest. He had to be a deputy of his.

Tipping his hat, Billy said, "Sheriff, good to see you."

"I have to say I wasn't expecting to see you so soon," Amherst said.

Billy dismounted and walked up to Amherst. He offered his hand and said, "Sheriff, what happened back at the house happened. I hope we're able to work together for the common good of this county and state."

Amherst took Billy's hand firmly in his and shook. "I suppose you'll be wanting to see what I found at the ambush site?"

"Yes, and I'd like to see the bodies," Billy said.

"Right this way," Amherst said, pointing towards his office.

Billy went in and looked around. On a table near the desk on the right sat an assortment of objects. He knew those had to be the items found because one of the pistols was Hemsworth's. He took the pistol in his hand and ran his fingers over it.

"That's one of three I found there," Amherst said.

His deputy came in and took a seat at the desk on

the left.

"It belonged to Marshal Hemsworth. I'll be taking it with me," Billy said and slid it into his waistband.

"Nothing really there that tells me anything about those men," Amherst said.

Unfortunately, Amherst was correct.

"Were the horses there?" Billy asked.

"Two horses, one belonged to the marshal and the other to one of the men who ambushed you. As you can see, nothing of value to tell us who these men were," Amherst said.

"Have you looked into who Joseph Paul King is?" Billy asked as he fingered through the items and trinkets.

Amherst gave his deputy a quick look and said, "I just found out. He's a wanted man. There's a warrant out for his arrest in three states for murder. He's a hired gun, a contract killer. He goes by the name Killer Joe."

"That's original," Billy snarled. "Where's he from?"

"He's originally from Canada," Amherst replied.

Billy stopped what he was doing and turned. "Canada?"

"Yes."

"Al Cummins is from Canada too. Was there any identity on the other man?"

"Nothing, wait, wait," Amherst said. "In the tin on the table, there's coins in it. I believe they're Canadian coins."

Billy saw the brass tin, popped the top, and saw the assortment of coins. He fished through and found the Canadian coins Amherst had mentioned. "Could be coincidental, or it may not be."

"Marshal, are you thinking now that the attack against you wasn't random but planned? Were they trying to rescue Al Cummins?" Amherst asked.

"I'm thinking that's a real possibility. Sheriff, where's your telegraph office?" Billy asked.

"Down the street on the left," Amherst said.

"I need to send an urgent telegram, but first I need to write something down," Billy said.

"On my desk there," Amherst said, pointing to the desk on the right.

Billy found a pencil and paper and jotted down an address. He handed it to Amherst and said, "Gather all of Marshal Hemsworth's personal effects and ship them to this address. It's his home in Idaho. And can you arrange for his body to be sent back too?"

The door to the office opened and in came a young man; he wore a black visor and bow tie with a black vest over a crisp white long-sleeve shirt. On the brim of his nose hung a pair of wire-rim glasses. "Sheriff, I have an urgent telegram from the United States Attorney in Missoula."

Billy's ears perked up, and he wondered what the US Attorney would want with Amherst.

"Give it here, son," Amherst said.

The clerk stepped forward, his chest heaving, as he'd run from the telegraph office. "Here, sir, I came as soon as it came across with the header to get into your hands immediately."

Amherst took the telegram, unfolded it and read.

The expression on his face went blank. He looked up to the clerk and said, "Thank you for bringing this over." He dug into his pocket and found a coin; he tossed it to the clerk.

Happy with his tip, the clerk exited the office.

"What does the US Attorney in Missoula want?" Billy asked, sensing it had something to do with Al.

"I sent a message to the marshals' office in Missoula after I found Marshal Hemsworth's body and heard about you. I thought it best to inform them of the situation. I planned on telling you but hadn't had a chance."

"Okay," Billy said, finding no fault in that practical decision.

"However, I wasn't expecting a message like this in return," Amherst said, holding the telegram out for Billy to read.

Stepping forward, Billy took the telegram and read. As his eyes passed over the words, his heart rate began to increase. When he was finished, he turned away from Amherst and stared outside. He spotted Alice pacing back and forth, no doubt waiting for him to emerge.

"Marshal, it appears there's nothing to be done," Amherst said.

"This is wrong. Something is very wrong," Billy snapped.

"I would agree, it all seems to be a bit odd, but you read it, as I did. We're to stand down from pursuing Al Cummins."

"He's a murdering scoundrel, and we can't just let him get away," Billy barked, spinning back around, his eyes wide with rage.

"Those instructions aren't just for you, they're for me. We're to do nothing about him and anyone who's in his company, who we have to assume is Killer Joe," Amherst said.

"Stop reminding me what the damn telegram said. I read it too!"

"Will you be going back to Idaho?" Amherst asked.

"I'm not going anywhere. I'm going to go looking for Al Cummins and those other men," Billy declared.

"But the telegram ordered you back to Idaho, and to take Marshal Hemsworth's body with you," Amherst said.

Billy crumpled up the paper and threw it on the floor. "I don't care what they say. Those men are a menace and need to be stopped. You don't have to join me, I don't care, just don't get in my way."

"Marshal Connolly, are you sure that is wise?" Amherst asked.

Billy picked up his hat from the desk and headed for the door. Before exiting, he turned and said, "Sheriff, please forward all of Marshal Hemsworth's personal effects and his body to that address I gave you, and forward a message to his wife informing her to expect it."

"But you—"

Interrupting him, Billy asked, "Sheriff, can you please do that for me?"

Amherst nodded and said, "I can. It's the least I can do."

"Thank you," Billy said. He opened the door and walked out.

Hearing the door open and close, Alice spun around. "There you are. Are you done?"

"I am," Billy said, walking to his horse.

Seeing that he looked agitated, she asked, "What's happened?"

"Your sheriff is worthless."

"I told you that in so many words."

"As are my superiors. Actually, my superiors could be more; they could be corrupt," Billy said, unhitching his horse.

"Tell me, what's happened?"

Billy gritted his teeth. He didn't want to involve her, but he had no one to turn to. "I've been ordered back to Coeur d'Alene, and the sheriff has been told to stand down from pursuing Al or Killer Joe."

"I don't understand," Alice said, shocked by the news.

"I don't understand either," Billy said. He mounted the horse and waited for her.

She got atop her horse and asked, "What will you do?"

"They've left me no choice but to disobey their orders. Those men killed my friend and your sister, as well as committed other unspeakable acts, and it appears they're aligned with Al. I cannot in good conscience turn and run knowing that those men are out there. I need to hunt them down and give them the justice that is sorely lacking."

"Can I come with you?" she asked.

"Sheriff, Sheriff, help," a boy hollered, running up to

Billy.

Looking down, Billy could see the fear in the boy's face. "What is it?"

"My family, they've been murdered, and my little brother, he's been taken prisoner," the boy said, out of breath.

Billy looked towards the sheriff's office, debating if he should tell Amherst, then decided against it. There was something about Amherst he didn't trust. He gave in too easily, he had murderers and cutthroats in his county killing, but he would only do the bare minimum. Feeling that the boy had mistaken his badge for him being the sheriff, he wasn't going to tell him otherwise. "Where did this happen?"

"Just about six miles southwest of town, just off the road to Missoula. Come, please hurry," the boy said.

"It's them, isn't it?" Alice asked.

"I think there's a good chance," Billy said. "You said you know this area like the back of your hand."

"I do," Alice said.

"Good, then you're coming with me, but only to help if I need it. You're to stay behind if things go sideways," Billy said.

Alice thought about protesting, but this was her opening and she was going to take it. "Okay."

Looking back to the boy, Billy said, "What's your name?"

"Clive," the boy answered.

Billy offered his hand and said, "Clive, hop on. Let's go save your brother."

SIX MILES SOUTHWEST OF GREAT FALLS, MONTANA

Clive pointed down the road and said, "I live in the cabin just off the road on the right about a quarter mile, Sheriff."

"I think I should tell you I'm not the sheriff, but I am a United States Marshal," Billy confessed.

"That's about the same, isn't it?" Clive asked, confused about the distinction.

"We're both lawmen, but as far as me being the same as your sheriff, I'd say we're quite different," Billy said.

"What are you going to do?" Alice asked.

"Clive, what's the layout of your land? How does the cabin sit, and is there a good place to hide and watch?" Billy asked.

"Yes, go around and come in from the back. There's only a single window, so you can walk up to the cabin unseen if you come up on the right side of it. There's a trail not far off this way, just take it west, and you'll end up there," Clive said, pointing into the forest to his right.

"How many men did you see?" Billy asked.

"Two, I think," Clive answered.

"I want you two to hide off the road here in the trees. I'm going to head down and check out the cabin," Billy said, dismounting. He paused a moment once he put his feet on the ground, as the pain from his wound reminded him it was there. He pulled his Winchester rifle from its scabbard and handed the reins to Clive.

"I can help," Alice said.

"You can help by keeping him safe," Billy said.

Alice grunted her displeasure.

Billy looked at the area and felt a sense of déjà vu. "This looks familiar. I believe we were ambushed not too far down the road. I rode past here on my way to your house." He looked back over his shoulder in the direction they'd just come and said, "The fork to the right leads to your house, correct?"

"Yes," Alice said.

"I wonder why they didn't go far. Maybe they're wounded," Billy mused.

"Let's hope so," Alice said.

"Marshal, please hurry. My brother needs you," Clive said.

"I'm going, and don't you worry, I'll get your brother back safely," Billy promised.

"You're one man. You can't possibly arrest them all," Alice said.

Billy gave her a crooked smile and said, "Who said anything about arresting anyone?"

A rustling in the trees to their left alerted them to someone or something coming.

Billy pulled and cocked his pistol.

Alice did the same.

As the sound grew louder and more distinct, they could tell it was a person walking.

Billy stepped forward and got in front of the others, who were still in the saddle.

The heavy footfalls continued.

Billy's index finger rested on the trigger. If the

person meant them harm, he could squeeze it in less than a second.

A groan came from the woods. "Help."

It was a man's voice. Billy stepped towards the edge of the woods and called out, "Who's there?"

"Help," the man's voice called out.

Billy's grip tightened on his pistol and his breathing slowed.

Out from a thick shrub the man emerged. It was Henry, his clothing was stained with blood, and his ashen appearance told Billy that he'd been wounded severely.

Recognizing him, Billy barked, "Hands up!"

"Help, please," Henry cried out, his voice weak.

Billy advanced on Henry. When he got within arm's length, he reached out with his left hand and threw him down.

Henry hit the ground hard and fell over.

"Where are the rest of you?" Billy asked, his pistol leveled at Henry's face.

"I don't know. Help me, please," Henry moaned.

Billy dropped to a knee and put the muzzle of his pistol against Henry's forehead and said, "Where is Al?"

"I...don't...know," Henry replied.

"You ambushed me and my partner. He's dead now. I need you to tell me who ordered this, and where are the others?" Billy snapped.

Henry coughed loudly, his eyes rolled back into his head, and he let out a gasp.

"Is he..." Alice asked.

"I don't know," Billy replied. He put two fingers to

his neck to check, and felt a pulse. "He's alive."

Henry's eyes opened wide. He stared at Billy and with a raspy tone said, "Help me."

"Where are the others?" Billy asked again.

"I don't know," Henry answered once more. "I was shot. I came to and was all alone on the road. I saw Gus; he was dead, as was that marshal…"

Pressing his muzzle harder into Henry's forehead, Billy snapped, "That marshal was my partner and my friend."

"I'm sorry, I didn't know," Henry replied.

"Where are the others? I'm getting tired of asking," Billy said, his anger rising.

Alice dismounted and slowly walked towards the two men, her fingers wrapped firmly around her pistol's grip.

"I'm going to count to three, and you'd better tell me where the others are, or I'll put an end to your life," Billy threatened. He was so focused on Henry that he didn't notice Alice walking up.

"I don't know. I woke and I was alone. They left me," Henry said, his voice straining.

Alice reached the men, leveled her pistol at Henry, and said, "You raped my ma and grandma."

Henry looked up and saw Alice. He didn't recognize her on account that he never saw her that night. "Ma'am, I don't know what you're talking about."

Surprised to see her standing there, Billy said, "It's probably best you take a few steps back."

Ignoring Billy, she said again, "You raped my ma and grandma that night. You came to my house asking for shelter then returned later."

"I don't know what you're talking about, ma'am," Henry lied.

Billy pushed down on his pistol, digging the muzzle deeper into Henry's forehead. "Answer the girl honestly."

"It wasn't my idea. It was Gus and Joseph; they came up with the idea," Henry said.

"So you were there?" Alice asked.

"I was, but I-I'm sorry, I'm so sorry. Can't you see I'm hurt? I need help," Henry cried.

Billy shot Alice a look and could see the determination in her eyes. "Don't do it."

"You were there, you mentioned Joseph and Gus, but I saw a fourth man that night the first time you came. Where is he?" Alice asked.

The news of a fourth man was a surprise to Billy.

"Harry, you're talking about Harry. He didn't come back. He disagreed with what Gus and Joseph had planned, so we tied him up. He never came to your house that night," Henry confessed.

"Where is Harry?" Billy asked.

"He's dead. Joe killed him," Henry said.

"Who hired you?" Billy asked.

Alice kept her eyes glued on Henry, and her anger kept rising. She leaned closer with her pistol out in front of her.

Catching her move, Billy again said, "Don't do it. He can answer questions that I need answers to."

Unable to control her emotional state, she pulled the trigger. A .36-caliber round blasted from the barrel and slammed into Henry's face.

He let out a quick yelp, choked on the blood that was flowing from the hole in his face, and died.

Billy jumped back and said, "What the hell?" He stood and said, "Why did you do that? He could have helped us."

"He was a murderer and rapist, but he was telling you the truth; he doesn't know where the others are," Alice said.

Billy uncocked his pistol and holstered it. "I don't know why I brought you along."

"All you were doing was talking and talking. I gave him what he deserved," Alice said.

***

Upon hearing the crack of the gunshot, Joseph jumped to his feet. He opened the door slightly and peered out.

Al rolled over and asked, "Was that a gunshot?"

"Yeah," Joseph said, scanning the front yard. He glanced to Adam and asked, "You were lyin' yesterday, were you?"

"No, sir," Adam said.

Joseph shut the door and raced over to Al and said, "Can you ride?"

Struggling to sit up, Al said, "I don't think so. It still hurts so bad and I'm burning up."

"Boy, do you have a wagon?" Joseph asked.

"Yes, sir, along the side of the house," Adam said.

Joseph scooped Al up and cradled him in his arms.

"Open the door," he ordered Adam, who did what he asked without question. Outside, he rushed with Al in his arms and made his way to the side of the house, and just as Adam had said, there was a wagon. He laid Al in the back and raced to get his horse. He brought it back and hitched it to the wagon. Running back inside, he gathered their belongings, and on his way out he saw Adam. "It's your lucky day, kid. I'm not taking you with me."

Adam said nothing. He stared at Joseph and prayed for him to leave.

Joseph gave Adam a wink and ran to the wagon. He threw everything in the bed of the wagon and hopped on. Looking over his shoulder, he asked, "How ya doing, Al?"

"I've been better," Al said.

Joseph whipped the reins. The horse lurched forward. Slowly the wagon pulled away and onto the road.

"Where to now?" Al asked.

"Away from here, far away from here," Joseph said.

***

Billy turned the cabin upside down, looking for anything that could be a clue as to where Al and Joseph had gone, but found nothing.

When he'd arrived at the cabin, he found Adam lying next to his parents' dead bodies, holding his mother's hand. The scene was touching and only validated his search for the outlaws.

166

"There's nothing that tells me where they went," Billy said.

"I spoke with Adam. He said they left twenty minutes ago in a wagon. They can't be too far ahead," Alice said.

"Twenty minutes ago was also the time you shot that man," Billy barked.

Not liking that Billy was yelling at her, she snapped back, "I might have made a mistake by doing that, but I had to. He raped my mother and my grandmother."

Billy thought about coming back with a rebuttal but decided against it. He'd made his point, and now he needed to get back in the saddle again. He stepped around Alice and made his way to his horse. He tightened the saddle strap and saddlebags because if he was going to catch them, he'd have to ride hard and fast.

Alice did the same thing to her horse.

Seeing what she was doing, he said, "You're not coming with me."

"I am because I know this county, you don't," she said.

"We had them, they were here, but they got away," Billy complained. He pulled out his pocket watch and checked the time. "Eight more hours of daylight; there's plenty of time to catch them."

"There's a triple fork in the road about three miles down. What we don't know is which way they went," Alice said.

"They're in a wagon. I can track them easily," Billy said confidently.

"But what if they went off the road?" Alice asked.

"I'll be able to see that. I need you to take these boys to town and inform the sheriff about what's occurred. That might get him off his ass to help," Billy said.

The heavy sound of horses sounded on the road just beyond.

Billy and Alice looked. It was Amherst and his deputy.

"What are the odds of that?" Billy said, a smirk on his face.

Amherst spotted them and rode up. "Marshal, I've reconsidered."

"How did you know we'd be here?" Billy asked.

"I knew you headed southwest out of town. I suspected you might ride out to the ambush site, and I look over, and here you are," Amherst said. "What are you doing here anyway?"

"These boys," Billy said, nodding to Clive and Adam, "their parents were murdered by Joseph and Al."

Amherst gasped and said, "Damn it."

"Sheriff, I won't say anything about what happened before, but right now we have a chance to catch these men and put an end to their killing," Billy said.

"I agree, so I'm offering to help, along with my deputy here. His name is Rob Ellis," Amherst said.

Billy nodded to Rob and said, "The more to help, the better."

"I'm going with you too," Alice said.

Amherst gave Alice a peculiar look and asked, "Is this true?"

"No, it's not. She joined me here only because…well, I made a mistake," Billy said.

"I want to go. I need to go," Alice declared.

"No, and that is it. I have the sheriff and Rob now to help, and they know this county better than you. I'm sorry, Alice, this is where your ride ends," Billy said. Turning to Amherst, he continued, "We're wasting daylight. Killer Joe and Al fled the cabin here in a wagon about thirty minutes ago. They were seen heading that way."

"We can catch them if we go now," Amherst said.

"Agreed," Billy said. "Alice, please take these boys somewhere safe. Maybe your house or the church in town until we can locate some relatives."

Alice grunted her disapproval.

"Sheriff, shall we?" Billy asked.

"Let's ride," Amherst said.

The three men bolted away and quickly disappeared out of sight.

Clive walked over to Alice and asked, "Where will you be taking us?"

Still fuming over being left behind, Alice felt defiant. She gave Clive a harsh look and replied, "I know you know how to ride a horse, correct?"

"Yes."

"Do you know where the north fork is up ahead a few miles?"

"Yes," Clive replied.

"See that horse there?" Alice asked.

"Yes, I see it," Clive answered.

"You're gonna take that horse. You and your brother are going to ride up to the fork, take the right, head a few miles down. On the right just past Sutter's Creek, you'll see a farmhouse in the distance. That's my house. Go there and tell my ma or grandma that I sent you. My ma might give you some grief, but if you give her this," she said, pulling two bottles of whiskey from her saddlebags and handing them to him, "she'll be fine. Tell her I sent you and that she's to take care of you. Feel free to tell her what happened to your parents. She might come off harsh at first, but she'll have sympathy. Do you understand?"

"I do, but I have a question," Clive said.

"What's that?" Alice asked.

"Can we bury my parents first?" Clive asked.

Hearing that tore at her emotions. She felt their pain and pledged that what she was doing wasn't just for herself but for them too. "Of course, bury them, pay what respects you need to, then ride to my house."

"Yes, ma'am," Clive said.

"I'm not a ma'am; I'm only seventeen," Alice said. She put her foot in the stirrup and pulled herself onto the back of the horse. "Now you're sure you can do as I ask?"

"Of course, my pa always said I was mature for my age," Clive said, the bangs of his dirty-blond hair covering his eyes when the breeze swept in.

"Your pa was right; I can see it in your eyes. You're not only mature but brave. You ran all the way to town to tell someone. You risked everything for your brother,"

Alice said.

Looking over at Adam, who sat on a stump outside the cabin, fiddling, he said, "He's my only family now."

Those words stung her. With Martha gone, she didn't have another sibling to share the rest of her life with. There was no one left to talk about things that girls talk about or discuss babies and the best way to bake a pie. It not only saddened her but brought out a rage that had showed itself not an hour ago when she killed Henry. She couldn't rest until she knew each man responsible was dead. Looking towards the road, she said, "Clive, you take care."

"I will, but can I ask where you're going?"

"I'm going to go kill a man," she replied.

TEN MILES SOUTHWEST OF GREAT FALLS, MONTANA

"Stop!" Al cried out, his body bouncing up and down with each bump in the road.

"I can't!" Joseph replied, whipping the horse to go faster.

"Stop, I can't take it!" Al shouted. The pain from the infected wound had only gotten worse. The cauterization hadn't done anything but seal the infection inside his body. His fever had risen and the infection was spreading.

"Al, you're going to have to suffer. We're already going slow as it is. I have to assume they're on our tail," Joseph said.

"No, stop!" Al shouted.

"No, I won't."

"Stop!" Al shrieked.

Having heard enough, Joseph pulled back on the reins and brought the wagon to a full stop. He spun around and snapped, "Shut up. I can't even hear myself think."

Sweat poured off Al's face, and his clothes were soaked. "I can't do this. I don't want to go on."

"That's foolish talk."

Al lifted up his shirt and said, "Look, look at it." The area around the wound on Al's belly had spread. The epicenter was black where the poker had burnt his skin, and out from there it was a mix of red and purple. "It's worse. I fear I'm not going to make it, and I don't want to suffer in my last moments."

"Your talk is foolish. Now we can't wait too much longer."

"You don't even know if we're being followed. All we heard was a single gunshot; it could have been someone hunting."

Looking in the direction they'd just come, Joseph could sense they were being chased. "Someone's coming; I can feel it."

"Why?"

"Why what?"

"Why did you come to rescue me? We haven't seen each other in a decade; now you feel a sense of obligation. What's the real reason?" Al asked.

"Does there need to be a reason outside of the fact

that you're my friend?"

"Joe, you don't have friends. Yes, we were friends when we were kids, but you left and went your own way. You became a contract killer, you're Killer Joe, and Killer Joe doesn't have friends, so why is it you came?"

"I came because you're my friend."

"Did you come thinking I had money somewhere? 'Cause if you did, I'm here to tell you that I don't. All that money I defrauded people out of is gone. I'm broke; I don't have a secret stash of cash somewhere."

Joseph's facial expression shifted. He looked like a child when someone told them that Santa Claus didn't exist.

"I can see it in your face; you thought I had some vast fortune hidden away. I don't. Those were all stories, lies. I liked hearing them because it made me sound bigger than I was, but there is no fortune, no money hidden. All the money I stole is gone," Al confessed.

"There's nothing?"

"Did you come hoping to get your hands on that?"

"I came hoping that..." Joseph said before pausing. His thoughts swirled about how to respond.

"Joe, just leave me here. If someone is chasing us, let them come. I'll hold them off as long as I can to give you more time to flee."

"You'd do that?"

"Of course, even though you came with hopes of getting your filthy hands on my money, I'll do what's right for an old friend," Al said.

"You said I don't have friends," Joseph said, his tone

somber.

"No, you don't. You're a damn killer, but were you and I friends once? Yes, we were, but we changed. You know I'm right. I am grateful for all you did even though you did it with hopes of putting your grubby hands on my money."

"I did want to help you though, that's not a lie."

"Now go, leave, but give me a pistol," Al said.

Joseph hopped down from the wagon and leaned over the side. He took Al's hand and said, "Thanks for telling me."

"If we're being chased, you'll never get away hauling me around. Unhitch the horse and go. Get out of here."

Joseph nodded and did as Al said. He unhitched the horse, threw his saddle and saddlebags on its back, and readied himself to ride off. He found a spare pistol in his bags, confirmed it was loaded, and handed it to Al. "Here."

Al took it with his trembling hands.

"You're sure about this?" Joseph asked.

"Would you still take me if I changed my mind, after knowing I don't have any money?"

"Yeah."

"Liar. Now get, go," Al said.

Joseph tipped his hat and said, "See you on the other side."

"Goodbye, Joe."

Joseph mounted his horse and took off without taking a second glance back. He raced down the trail to the south, unsure where he'd go next. After ten minutes of hard riding, he exited the trees, and before him were grass-covered hills. He didn't know where to go. He could keep heading south, but go where? He was disappointed that he'd come all this way with hopes of getting his hands on Al's money only to come up empty-handed. His disappointment soon turned to anger that after so much trouble and effort, he was leaving worse than when he started, having lost his father's pocket watch at the house back in Great Falls. A strong temptation to go back and get it gripped him. He knew the dangers entailed in doing something like that, but it would most likely be the last place they'd look for him. Then again, he could be found. The safer bet was to keep heading south, but this was Killer Joe, and playing it safe wasn't his modus operandi.

***

Seeing the wagon in the road ahead, Billy cried out, "Hold up."

Amherst and Rob pulled back on their horses hard.

With twenty feet now separating them from the wagon, Billy said, "Something isn't right here. Keep your eyes peeled."

"Rob, advance and see if anything is in the wagon," Amherst ordered.

Nervous, Rob gulped but did as he was told. He trotted forward enough to eye the back of the wagon. "There's a man lying in the back. He's not moving."

Billy advanced, stopping where Rob was. He looked

and said, "It's Al."

"Well, is he dead?" Amherst asked, still at the spot where he'd stopped.

"I'll go find out," Rob said, riding up until he was alongside the wagon.

"Be careful," Billy said, his pistol now in his hand.

Rob pulled his pistol and cocked it. He rode once around the wagon, but he didn't see any movement. "He doesn't look like he's breathing."

"Where's Joe?" Billy asked, his eyes scanning the wooded area.

Amherst made his way up to Billy and said, "He could be anywhere now that he's on a horse."

"Damn!" Billy grunted.

"Let's see if there's anything in the wagon," Amherst said, moving towards the wagon. "Rob, get down and search it."

Rob dismounted and went to the edge of the wagon. He looked inside and began shifting through the few items in it. He reached towards Al but stopped in horror when Al opened his eyes and raised a cocked pistol at him.

"Hello there, Deputy," Al said, then pulled the trigger.

Rob's head snapped back when the .45-caliber round passed through it, blowing out the back of his head. He dropped where he stood.

Amherst's horse reared and almost threw him off.

Al sat up, cocked his pistol, aimed at Amherst, and fired.

The round struck Amherst in the side and was enough to topple him off his horse. He hit the ground hard with a thud.

Al wasn't done. He cocked the pistol again and hollered, "Die, you son of a bitch lawman." He took aim on Amherst, who was scrambling on the ground, and fired. Like his other shots, this one was accurate too. It hit Amherst in the top of his head and nearly took off his scalp.

Amherst grunted then fell over dead.

Pivoting to engage Billy, Al cocked the pistol once more, but before he could fire this time, Billy had sent a round towards him.

The .45-caliber round from Billy's Colt penetrated Al's upper chest and exited between his shoulder blades.

The pain was excruciating. Al coughed heavily and spat out blood.

Unafraid, Billy advanced, his pistol cocked and ready. He closed in on Al, his pistol leveled at him, and just before he pulled the trigger, he said, "I've been waiting to do this."

Al was choking on blood, his eyes wide with terror, as he knew this was it, this was how he was going to die.

Billy saw that Al wasn't going to fire anymore, so he drew closer until he was a few feet away. "Die, you son of a bitch!" Billy said, pulling the trigger.

Al's head snapped back when the round blasted through it. He let out a grotesque groan and fell over, his head hitting the side of the wagon.

The heavy sounds of a horse riding up on him struck fear in Billy. He imagined it was Joseph coming to kill him. He cocked his pistol, spun around, and pointed towards the sound of the horse. With his finger on the trigger applying pressure, he gazed over the top of the barrel and saw it was not Joseph but Alice. He lowered the pistol and called out, "What the hell are you doing here?"

She rode up, surveyed the scene, and asked, "Are they dead?"

"Yeah, all of them," Billy replied. "Now tell me, why aren't you caring for those boys?"

"They're fine. I needed to come. I'm so close to killing another man who was responsible for what happened to my family," she explained.

"I told you to stay with the boys, make sure they're taken care of, not follow us," Billy barked.

She rode over to the wagon and peeked inside. "Is this Al Cummins?"

"Yes."

"Then the last person we need to get is Joseph Paul King."

"There's no we in this. You need to go home."

Alice shot him a harsh look and said, "You need me. Look at you. You let one man kill two lawmen."

"I didn't let anyone do anything. He looked dead."

Alice smirked and said, "So he played possum, huh?"

"This isn't funny," Billy said.

"Where's Joseph?"

"I have no idea. He could be anywhere now," Billy said, his frustration showing through.

"What are we waiting for? Let's go after him."

"Go where? He's on horseback, with a twenty-minute or more head start. He could literally be anywhere now."

"But we have to try."

"Where should we go? You choose," Billy said, clearly annoyed.

"Maybe he's going…" she said, looking around. "He wouldn't head back to town, that wouldn't make sense, so he could be…"

"Going anywhere else, north, south, west, and, yes, he could be doubling back east and going back around town then off to Canada."

"You're the marshal. Where would he go?" Alice asked.

"I don't know. I don't know who he is; I don't know anything about him. I've got a dead sheriff and deputy, and Al Cummins, the man I was escorting back to the authorities in Canada, is also dead. This entire thing has been a damn nightmare."

"You're saying we should give up?" Alice asked, shocked.

"No, I never give up," he said, taking a breath. "Let's head south."

"So I'm coming with you?"

"Yes, on account that you being with me is safer for you than not. Now let's ride," Billy said and took off at a full gallop.

A smile stretched across Alice's face. She was officially a member of a posse; at least that was what she'd describe it as. Happily she raced off to catch up to him.

SOUTH CASCADE COUNTY, TWENTY-TWO MILES SOUTH OF GREAT FALLS, MONTANA

Billy slowed his horse to a stop. He scanned the rolling hills to the south, the shadows of the trees and shrubs growing long as the sun closed in on the western horizon. They'd ridden for miles and miles yet found no sign of Joseph, meaning they would probably never find him. Frustrated and tired, he pulled out a canteen, pulled the plug, and took a drink.

Alice rode up alongside him, wiped her brow with her sleeve, and said, "This is the furthest I've ever been from home."

Handing her the canteen, he said, "Congratulations."

She took the canteen and tipped it back.

"I normally wouldn't suggest this, but I think we should turn around and head back," he said.

"So we're giving up?" she asked.

"I don't have a choice. He's liable to be anywhere. Just one deviation off his trail and the farther we go past that puts us miles and miles away from him."

"I don't want to go home, not yet."

"I need to get you back to your mother or I'll be arrested for kidnapping," he joked.

She took another drink from the canteen and handed it back to him. Laughing, she said, "My ma will probably try to have you arrested."

"I'm sorry we couldn't find him."

"I'm sorry we couldn't find him, either," she said. "It's just not fair that he gets to murder and rape and not face consequences."

"He'll get his one day, I know that, but I hear what you're saying," Billy said, stowing the canteen back in his saddlebag. He rubbed the neck of his horse and said, "How about we give the horses a break, feed them, and then head back?"

Not hesitating, she dismounted and stretched. "I hurt all over."

"If you've never been this far, then I suppose you would be sore," he said, climbing down off his horse. He took a stake from his saddlebag and shoved it into the ground. Taking the reins of his horse, he tied them around the stake then removed the saddle.

She followed what he did.

He took a feedbag from his saddlebag and secured it to his horse's head. "I'll have him feed for a bit; then we'll get your horse fed."

She nodded. Seeing a large boulder a few feet away, she walked over and sat down on a flat part of it.

He walked over and sat next to her. "I didn't tell you, but I lost my father too."

"What happened to him?"

"He got sick. It happened right after we moved to Idaho."

"You're not from there?" she asked, genuinely curious.

"No, I was born in Ireland. We moved when I was fourteen."

"You're from Ireland? How come I don't hear an accent?"

"On account that I didn't think a US Marshal should sound like an Irishman," he confessed.

"Say something with your accent," she urged.

"I'm not even sure I can anymore." He laughed.

"Please."

He cleared his throat and said with a thick Irish accent, "Top of the mornin' to ya."

"I love it." She squealed with laughter. "You should sound like that more often."

"I don't think so. No one really knows me that way except my family, and I don't think it's a good idea to confuse them," he explained.

"I'd love to go to Ireland. Heck, I'd love to go anywhere but Montana," she said. Opening her arms wide, she continued. "I want to see the world. I've read about the ocean. I'd love to see it. Have you seen it?"

"Of course I've seen it. I sailed across it to get to America."

"That's true. How was it?"

"Vast, I didn't see land for two weeks," he replied.

"I so want to see it, walk on a beach, get my toes stuck in the sand."

"One day I'm sure you'll do just that," he said. Seeing his horse shake its head, he went to it, removed the feedbag, and tossed in more. He slung it over her horse's head and returned to the rock.

Alice was now lying down staring at the darkening sky. The sun had set on the far westerly side of the mountains.

"We can leave as soon as your horse has eaten," he said.

"Speaking of food, do you have any?"

"I think so."

"I'm so tired. Could we sleep here tonight then head back?" she asked.

While sleeping close to her was tempting, he said, "I need to get you back."

"I don't think I'll be able to make the ride, especially at night. I'm exhausted."

"I'm sure your mother is already concerned. I don't want to keep you out here any longer."

"Won't we get lost?" she asked.

He looked north and thought that could be a possibility but didn't want to say it.

"Can we please just sleep here, get the rest we need after this long day, then head back in the morning?" she asked. "I want to sleep under the stars. I don't want this adventure to end."

"You think this is an adventure?"

"Yes, if you had lived my life, you would think the same way."

The hours of riding through the night didn't sound appealing, and he was also very tired and his side was aching badly. He could use the rest, and if they left just as the sun was rising, they'd reach her house by midafternoon.

She yawned loudly.

He gave her a smile and said, "Fine, we'll sleep here tonight, but we need to head back first thing."

"We're really going to sleep here?" she asked, sitting up, a look of pure excitement on her tender face.

"Yes, but we need to leave just before dawn."

She leaned over and hugged him. "Thank you."

Feeling uncomfortable yet enjoying the embrace, he said, "You're welcome."

"I don't have a bedroll."

"You can use mine. Go ahead and get it while I gather wood for a fire," he offered.

She raced to his saddle nearby.

He felt a surge of excitement about the idea, not because he had an ulterior motive, but he liked seeing her happy.

She returned with the bedroll under one arm and a small satchel on the other.

"You weren't lying, you don't want to go home," he said, amused by her excitement.

"If you had experienced what I had growing up, you wouldn't want to go back either."

"Maybe so."

"I can't thank you enough for first allowing me to join you," she said as she cleared a spot to lie down.

He stacked some wood and went to get his flint so he could start the fire. He returned to find her sitting on the bedroll, her legs pulled tight and humming a song. He was tempted to tease her, but he also found her behavior had an innocence that he found attractive. "I look at you sitting there, and I don't see the girl who just killed a man hours ago."

Her smile disappeared. "I'm not a girl, I'm a woman. I may not be eighteen yet, but soon I will be."

"Fair enough, but you don't seem disturbed by what happened earlier today."

She thought about his comment as she watched him get the fire going.

Silence fell over both of them as the fire caught and began to crackle. They stared at the dancing flames as the dark of night cast over them.

He opened his saddlebag and removed a canvas sack of hardtack and gave her a piece.

She took it and bit down. As she chewed, she kept thinking about his last comment. It struck her that it was an odd way of coping. She'd been through so much lately, yet she could still find a way to exude happiness, even innocent joy at the idea of sleeping outside, even though they were in the middle of pursuing a murderer.

"You've been quiet," he said.

"So have you."

"Was it what I said?" he asked, leaning back against his saddle.

"It was. I'm sure it seems quite peculiar that a young woman could easily kill a man."

"I've been thinking, and I suppose it's not so peculiar. What you did was justified in my eyes. He was guilty, so you did what would have happened if he'd been taken in."

"Some would say I murdered him, wouldn't they?" she asked.

"Some would, but who's ever going to know," Billy said. He took a bite of his hardtack and gave her a smile.

"I had to kill him, I can't explain it, but I didn't even look at him as a human being. He was an animal that needed to be put down," she said. "Whoever can do the things he did isn't a person but something worse. I don't regret it and never will; I just need to find one more."

"I told you we had a lot in common; well, we have a lot more than I let on," he said. "My ma too was raped. I saw the men leaving our house and followed them into town. There I confronted them and shot them both. Like you, I never had an ounce of regret. Never once have I thought back to that pivotal moment in my life and would take it back. Men who do those things are evil and need nothing short of killing."

"I'm glad you told me that."

"I understand your need to get every single one of the men who hurt your family, I do. But you must understand that I also have an obligation as a sworn lawman."

"What are you right now? Are you the man or the lawman?" she asked.

"Being that I'm out here against the orders of my superiors, I'd have to say I'm just a man."

"Will you go back to being a lawman?"

"Of course I will. This is just a detour," he said. "I'll be able to explain this without concern. It's horrible to say, but having the sheriff and his deputy dead is a good thing. No one but you knows I came out here against orders."

She crossed her heart with her finger and said, "I'll never say a word. Your secret is safe with me."

"I know it is," he said. "Listen, you'd best get some sleep. Dawn will come mighty fast."

She lay back and covered herself with a small wool blanket. Seeing that he was still sitting up, she asked, "What about you?"

"I'm going to stay up a bit. I've got a lot of thinking to do."

She gave him a smile and closed her eyes.

Billy stared into the flames, but his mind wandered. With his one chance gone at quickly finding Killer Joe, he'd have to regroup after taking Alice back home. But where should he begin looking? He didn't have an answer to any of the questions that troubled him, and didn't know when or if he ever would. The one thing he did know was that he'd never stop searching, no matter how long it took.

CHAPTER EIGHT

JULY 14, 1895

TWO MILES SOUTH OF GREAT FALLS, MONTANA

"Are you sure you don't want me to go with you?" Billy asked, looking towards Alice's house, which stood in the distance.

Sitting tall in her saddle, she answered confidently, "No, I need to do this alone. She'll just give you grief."

"But I should go help explain, don't you think?"

"No, please just go," she said, her tone signaling her disappointment at arriving home.

"I won't stop searching," he said, referring to finding Killer Joe. "I'll leverage everything to make sure he gets the justice he deserves."

"If you ever find out, can you please let me know?"

"I'll do that," Billy said, meaning every word of it. He found her alluring and didn't want their encounter to end, but it had to.

"Thank you, even though we didn't get him, I appreciate the adventure."

"No more thanking me," Billy said. He let out a sigh and continued, "I've got to get the sheriff's and deputy's bodies back into town and inform the mayor what happened."

"I can help," she offered.

"No, you go back and tell your ma that I apologize for taking you away."

"I won't do that. I'm going to tell her the truth."

A silence fell between them; neither wanted to say goodbye.

"I should let you go," Alice said timidly.

"Yes, I really need to go get the sheriff," he said and turned his horse around.

"Marshal—" she said before being interrupted.

"Call me Billy, please."

"Billy, if you're ever close by, don't hesitate to stop by and say hello," she offered.

He looked down shyly and said, "I can do that, but I can't promise when that'll be."

"I understand."

"Ah, maybe you'll allow me to write you. Can I do that?"

Her expression shifted from sadness to joy. "Yes, of course."

He then wanted to ask her if she'd be available to court but found himself questioning that thought. They lived hundreds of miles apart, and the idea just seemed foolish. He immediately dashed the idea and said, "I'll send you letters letting you know how things are going with the search for Killer Joe."

"I'll look forward to them."

Again an awkward silence fell over them.

He nodded and said, "Goodbye and take care,

Alice."

"Goodbye to you and safe travels, Billy."

The two gave each other one last look and rode their own separate ways.

***

Alice arrived back to the house, but instead of going straight in, she took her horse to the barn, unsaddled it, and ensured it had hay and feed to eat. Her mind raced with how to respond to her mother's endless questions and accusations that she knew were coming. She settled with just telling her the truth and nothing more. Soon she'd be eighteen; in fact, in three days she'd officially become an adult and could leave home if she saw fit without having to answer to her mother or anyone.

She headed across the yard to the house, her thoughts now filled with the adventures of the past two days and of Billy. She found him handsome, brave and strong-willed. The strong-willed part often clashed with her, but she found it forgivable. He was a man who acted that way not out of spite but out of an abundance of caution for her safety.

She scaled the back steps and entered the kitchen. When her eyes saw the scattered pans and debris, she froze. Something awful had happened while she was gone. She reached deep into the pocket of her skirt and removed the pistol. She thumbed the hammer back and held it out in front of her. She was tempted to call out, but if the person who had caused this was still in the house, the last thing she wished to do was alert them of her presence.

She carefully made her way to the door that separated the kitchen and the hallway, making sure to avoid stepping on anything that would make noise. She pressed her ear against the door and listened but heard nothing. She wondered if the boys had caused this mess or if they were even there. Slowly and cautiously she turned the knob and opened the door a crack. She peeked through to see the chaos continued on the other side.

A whimper sounded from upstairs.

She opened the door more to listen.

Without notice a hand reached in, grabbed the door, and threw it open fully. There stood Joseph. "Why, hello. We meet again."

Alice raised the pistol.

Joseph swung down with his pistol and struck her on the top of the head; it was similar to the way he'd hit Martha.

Alice stumbled backwards into the kitchen, only stopping when she hit the table. She dropped her pistol onto the floor, turned and took a step to run away.

Joseph wasn't going to allow her to flee this time. He burst into the kitchen, grabbed her arm, and swung her around. He reached back with his left hand and came forward, slapping her face with the back of his hand.

Her head snapped to the left.

He came back across her face, this time palm forward.

She crumpled to the ground, dizzy from the strikes.

Seeing the pistol in front of her, feet away, she reached for it.

He kicked the pistol out of reach, grabbed her by the back of her hair, and pulled her to her feet. "You're not getting away this time," he seethed.

Still able to think, she lashed out and clawed his face with her fingernails.

He bellowed in pain but didn't let go of his firm grip. He slammed her head down on the table; this time the blow to the head knocked her out.

Alice's body went limp and she fell to the floor.

"Let's pick up where we left off." He snickered.

***

Billy didn't get a quarter mile away when the urge to go back was so overwhelming that he turned around. He had met a unique and special woman, and if he didn't ask, he could lose her forever. In all the years he'd traveled, he never met someone like her, so to let her go now would be foolish.

He turned his horse around and rode for her house to ask if he could do more than write her; he wanted to see if he could court her. Yes, he knew that would entail discussing this with her mother, Maggie, and after what had happened recently, she could tell him to go away, but either way, he thought it best for Alice to know his true intentions were to see her in a romantic way.

He reached the drive and stopped when doubt and second thoughts came. What if she didn't feel the way he did? What if she said no? He now reconsidered, thinking that his overtures could be too much too soon.

"Just do it," he said. "But what if…"

Dismissing the fear and doubt, he decided to go for it, thinking that if he didn't tell her, he might never get a chance.

He rode down the drive fast, stopped just out front, and hopped off the horse. The second his feet touched the ground, his side reminded him that he was still healing. He sucked up the pain, straightened out his vest, and made for the front door, which sat open. He scaled the steps and stopped when he saw debris strewn inside as if it had been tossed about.

His senses kicked in and he felt something wasn't right. Not one to challenge his gut feelings, he pulled his pistol out slowly and thumbed back the hammer. He cleared the few feet to the edge of the doorway and leaned in to get a peek in the first room, to find the furniture was in disarray as if someone had thrown it here and there.

His heart was racing and his instincts were now screaming that someone not welcome was in the house. He stepped across the threshold and entered the house; pausing a foot inside, he let his ears listen for anything out of sorts.

It was quiet, too quiet. He knew Alice had only arrived minutes before, so she would have been moving about, and if her mother, Maggie, was here, he would have arrived to hear a litany of questions being lobbed in Alice's direction. Instead he was greeted with an eerie silence. He contemplated calling out, but something told him that was the last thing he wanted to do. He moved from the front room and into the hall, ensuring that each step he took was soundless. Ahead of him was the door that led to the kitchen, and to his left the base of the stairs stood.

He looked up the stairs but saw nothing, so he progressed into the kitchen to find it similar to the front room. He spun around and went to the door on the right. He turned the knob and pushed it open; it was a small office, and by the look of it, no one had used it in some time. With all of the rooms cleared, the only place left to go was upstairs. He found himself back at the base of the stairwell and stared up it. He recalled the floor plan of the second story and decided that upon reaching the second floor, he'd turn left and go to the first room; what he didn't know was it was Alice's.

He put his right foot down on the first step, lifted his left leg, and set that foot on the second step. The old steps creaked under his weight and sounded loud in the dead silence of the house. He set his foot on the third step, but this time paused to listen. He swore he heard a voice; it sounded as if it was muffled.

His grip on his pistol tightened and his heart rate increased. He listened, but the sound was gone. Was it a figment of his imagination? he thought, or had he really heard someone? The need to find Alice filled him with fear; his cautious behavior could possibly be putting her life in danger. So without any more regard, as swiftly and quietly as he could, he scaled the remaining steps but one.

Stopping just one step short of the second floor, he peered around the corner and looked down the darkened hallway, but saw nothing but three doors. Two of the doors were closed, one being Martha's room. The door to his left was also closed.

He stepped onto the landing, turned the knob on Alice's door, and pushed it open. There, huddled against the far wall, were Maggie, Anne, Clive and Adam; they were bound and had their mouths gagged.

Maggie whimpered and nodded with her head in the direction of the door.

Billy went to them and pulled Maggie's gag from her mouth.

"He's got Alice. He's got her at the barn!" Maggie cried.

Billy jumped to his feet. He turned and was paralyzed when he heard a scream coming from the backyard of the house. He knew it was Alice and she was in need. He spun around, exited the room, and raced down the stairs, through the kitchen and out the back. He instantly spotted someone running from the barn towards the house. He looked carefully and saw it was Alice, her clothes torn and a look of terror on her face.

Joseph emerged from the barn, a pistol tucked under his armpit as he buttoned his trousers. Blood dripped from his face and onto his white shirt.

Billy looked more carefully and recognized Joseph.

"I'm going to get you, bitch!" Joseph howled.

Alice had managed to flee Joseph's clutches by jabbing a hair comb into the side of his face. With that one blow, she pushed him off her and took flight. She knew if she could make it to the house, she could find something to defend herself with. She dashed towards the house, her mind only focused on survival, and happened not to see Billy until he stepped off the back porch. "Billy!" she cried out.

Springing into action, Billy raised his cocked pistol, aimed it at Joseph, and squeezed the trigger. His first round exploded from the barrel, traveled the fifty yards in less than a second, only to slam into the door of the barn, sending small wood fragments flying. He grunted, cocked his pistol again, and took aim.

Joseph looked back at the hole in the door, cocked his pistol, and aimed at Billy. He began to squeeze; then, just before he fired, he switched his aim to Alice and fired. His round hit Alice in the back.

She yelped in pain and toppled to the ground.

"No!" Billy cried out, seeing her fall. His sorrow turned to anger. He narrowed his gaze on the sights of his pistol, leveled them on Joseph's chest, and squeezed his second round off. This time his aim was true. The .45-caliber bullet slammed into Joseph's chest, hitting him just below his heart.

Joseph grunted from the impact and took two uneasy steps backwards. He looked down and saw the hole in his shirt. He could feel the warm blood flowing from the wound and see it soaking his shirt. "Son of a bitch," he said, shocked that he'd been shot.

Billy cocked his pistol, aimed like before, and squeezed off another round. Like the last time, this one hit just to the left of the previous shot.

Joseph recoiled from the second hit, dropped his pistol, and fell against the barn door. He slid down until he was on the ground. He coughed several times; a large amount of blood came up and spilled out of his mouth, landing on his shirt and trousers.

Seeing that Joseph was down, Billy made his way to Alice. He found her alive, but losing a lot of blood from the gunshot wound in her back, just above her waistline. He rolled her into his lap so she was looking up, and gazed into her eyes. "You're going to be alright. I've got you, and I'm going to fix you up, you hear me?"

"I've been shot."

"You have, but I think it's a clean wound like mine was," he said, seeing the exit hole in the front of her dress.

"It hurts," she said, her tone very matter of fact.

"Yes, getting shot does hurt," he said, almost wanting to laugh.

In the distance, Joseph grunted loudly and tried to rise.

Hearing Joseph, Billy lifted his head and looked to see Joseph attempting to get to his feet, but each time he tried to get up, he'd fall back down.

"I've gotta finish this," Billy said to Alice.

She nodded and said, "Do it for Martha."

"I'll do it for all of you," Billy said. He gently set her on the ground and got to his feet. He looked towards Joseph, and his expression shifted to rage. He marched over to Joseph, stopped feet away and said, "Today you die."

Using the latch on the door to steady himself, Joseph tried to get to his feet. Hearing Billy, he stopped, gave him a look and said, "I surrender. Take me in."

"Surrender?" Billy asked.

Joseph dropped to the ground, landing on his butt, raised his arms and said, "I surrender. Now arrest me and take me in. I need to see a doc."

Amused by Joseph's assumption, Billy said, "I'm not here to arrest you."

"You're going to kill me, an unarmed man?"

"Yes, I am."

"But you're a marshal; you're not supposed to kill unarmed people. You have to arrest me; now do it," Joseph said. "You're wearing the badge; you're a marshal, a lawman. You have to arrest me. I surrender."

Billy looked at the badge on his chest and smiled. He pulled it off and tossed it. "I'm not here as a marshal, I'm here as a man who is taking vengeance for all those you've harmed."

"You can't just do that," Joseph said. He hacked a few times and continued, "You have to follow the law."

A question popped into Billy's mind, so he asked without the anticipation of getting a straight answer from Joseph. "Who sent you?"

"I'll tell you after you take me to see a doc."

"I knew you'd answer like that," Billy said. He raised the pistol and aimed.

Holding up his hands, Joseph said, "Hold on, wait."

"Are you going to tell me what I want to know?"

"But you need to take me to see a doc and fast."

"Tell me," Billy said, "and I'll consider it."

"You have to take me to a doc. I'm dying here," Joseph whined.

"You can die with the answer to my question or take a chance that I'll arrest you and take you to town to see a doc in hopes that he'll patch you up."

Joseph spit out a large amount of blood, leaned his head back against the barn door, and said, "It was Al's father."

"What's his name?" Billy asked. "Where can I find him?"

"You don't know who he is?" Joseph asked, stunned by Billy's ignorance.

"No, I don't know who he is, so why don't you tell me."

"Can you lower the pistol first?"

Billy did as he said. "Who is he?"

"George Cummins is a judge. He's on the Supreme Court in British Columbia. He's a very powerful man," Joseph said. He started to cough heavily again. "Now that you know, please hurry and take me to a doc."

"It all makes sense."

"What makes sense?"

Joseph's question tore Billy away from his troubled thoughts. "I have one more question. Did you receive orders to attack us? Were you specifically told to kill us?" It was a question that he needed to know the answer to.

"Yes, we received a telegram that instructed us to do whatever was needed to save Al," Joseph confessed.

More troubling thoughts entered Billy's mind. The entire operation had been done to protect a powerful man's son. Al wasn't going back to Canada to be tried, he was going back to be protected, to be shielded from the law in the United States.

"Hey, are you going to take me?" Joseph asked, holding out his hand with hopes that Billy would help him to his feet.

Anger rose in Billy. If this was a setup, then the United States Attorney and others knew about it. They in many ways had sent him and Hemsworth on a mission without any regard for their safety. Did the United States government know that they'd be attacked? How high up did this go?

"I need to go see a doc!" Joseph barked.

Billy raised his pistol, aimed it at Joseph's gut and said, "This is for Martha." He pulled the trigger, unleashing a .45-caliber round.

Joseph howled in pain.

Billy cocked it and said, "This is for Alice." He fired another round into Joseph's stomach.

Joseph clenched his abdomen and cried out in pain.

Knowing he had one more round in the chamber, he cocked it and said, "And this is for my friend Marshal Hemsworth." Billy pulled the trigger, the hammer fell forward, and the pistol went off. This time he had aimed at Joseph's chest.

Joseph grabbed at the area, gagged for a second, then slumped over dead.

Billy stared at Joseph's dead body and felt a deep

sense of relief. He'd killed an unarmed man and had violated the very law he had sworn to uphold, but he didn't care. Joseph Paul King was a man who lived outside the law, so it seemed only right that he should die that same way. Killing Joseph was the right thing to do, and Billy would always know that sometimes there are righteous kills.

He holstered his pistol and made his way back to Alice, who still lay on the ground. He scooped her off the ground and carried her towards the house. "I'm going to fix you up, do you hear?"

Alice nodded.

"And when you're feeling better, I'm going to ask if you'll be open to me courting you."

Alice's eyes widened. She smiled and said, "I'd like that."

CHAPTER NINE

JULY 16, 1895

TWO MILES SOUTH OF GREAT FALLS, MONTANA

Billy waited patiently outside Alice's bedroom door, a bouquet of wildflowers in his right hand. Delicate footfalls sounded from the stairs.

Billy turned to see it was Adam. "How are you?"

"I'm good, Marshal," Adam answered. "Who are the flowers for?"

"Oh, these are for Miss Alice. You did know today is her birthday, didn't you?" Billy squatted down so he could be eye level with Adam and asked, "How's Maggie been to you?"

"Real nice. She's not had a drop of liquor since we came," Adam said.

"How do you know that?" Billy asked with a smile.

"She told us she gave it up; no more, she said," Adam answered. "She's repeated it many times."

"That's good news. Liquor can be a bad thing when you drink too much of it."

"I came up to check on Alice and to wish her a happy birthday."

"Well, Adam, that's what I'm doing here too," Billy

said. He tousled Adam's hair and gave him a wink.

The door creaked open and out stepped Doc Higgins, one of the local doctors from Great Falls. "If you'll excuse me," he said, his black case firmly in his grip.

"How's she doing?" Billy asked, a show of concern on his face.

Higgins stopped and gave Billy a quizzical look. "You're that marshal, aren't you?"

"I am," Billy answered.

"She'll be fine, just needs some rest and to have her bandage changed frequently; otherwise she'll heal just fine. As I explained to her mother, it's important to keep the wound clean so it doesn't fester."

"We'll make sure of that," Billy said.

Higgins removed his wire spectacles, wiped them off with a handkerchief, and put them back on. "There's a lot of talk about you in town."

"I'm aware," Billy said, referring to the buzz surrounding the sheriff being killed and the deaths of Al Cummins and Joseph King.

"I heard the mayor offered you the position of sheriff," Higgins said.

"He did; in fact, I just returned from meeting him in town."

"And? Will you be our new sheriff?"

"I will, but not right away. I have some other business to attend to, but upon my return, I'll be your new sheriff," Billy confirmed.

"Well, the rumors were that the mayor was offering

you the job. I'm happy you're taking it. I didn't much like the last one. I always found him to be a bit lazy and self-absorbed. Sad he died, but I am glad he's gone. They say you're sort of a hero around these parts."

"Not sure I'd call myself that. Anyway, is it safe to go inside and visit her?"

"Sure, sure, she's awake and talking, but she does need her rest."

"Thank you," Billy said. He turned to knock but stopped when Higgins spoke.

"Welcome to Great Falls…Sheriff."

"Thank you, Doc," Billy said, giving him a smile.

"Say, boy, I need some help. Do you mind carrying this downstairs and putting it in my wagon? I need to go visit the outhouse before I ride back to town," Higgins said to Adam.

"Sure thing," Adam said.

"Good boy," Higgins said, giving Adam his bag.

The two disappeared down the stairs.

Billy tapped on the door then opened it. Inside, he found Alice sitting up with Maggie by her side and Anne sitting in a chair at the foot of the bed. "Can I come in?"

"Yes, please," Alice said happily.

"Just for a minute, then she needs to get some sleep, doctor's orders," Maggie said.

Billy went to Alice's bedside, opposite Maggie. He gave her a big smile, handed her the flowers, and said, "Happy birthday."

Alice took the flowers and inhaled deeply. "Oh, they smell so sweet and they're beautiful, thank you."

"I just spoke with the doc. He says you'll be just fine," Billy said, hovering above the bed.

"I will," she said.

Maggie took the flowers and set them on the nightstand. "I'll get a vase later and put them in water for you." Giving Billy a skeptical look, she continued, "That was nice of you, Marshal."

"I saw the flowers and thought of Alice. Knowing it was her birthday, I thought they'd suffice as a nice gift," Billy said.

"They're perfect," Alice said.

The two locked in a gaze that told Anne and Maggie they could use some private time.

Getting up, Anne walked over to Maggie and nudged her. "Let's let these two talk…in private."

"But…" Maggie protested.

"Let's go see what the boys are doing," Anne said. "And you need to get a vase with water for those flowers."

Maggie's head swiveled back and forth between Anne and Alice. She gave Billy a look, sighed, and said, "Don't be long. She needs her rest."

Anne and Maggie left the room, but left the door cracked.

Alice glowed. If someone saw her, they wouldn't know she'd just been shot two days before. "Have a seat," she said, patting a spot next to her on the bed.

Billy sat and nervously looked at his hat and fiddled. "I'm glad you're doing well."

"Me too."

"I came to check on you and tell you that I'm leaving."

"Leaving? You're going back to Idaho?" she asked, her jovial expression melting away at the news of his departure.

"No, I'm going somewhere else. I'm not done tracking down everyone who had a part in this. I owe it to my partner."

"I understand. When will you return?"

"Soon, and it will be a permanent move," he said, wanting to give her hope that they could possibly be seeing more of each other.

"Permanent? You're moving to Great Falls?" she asked, her tone turning happy again.

"The mayor offered me the job of sheriff, and I just took it, so you're looking at the new sheriff of Great Falls," Billy answered. "However, I won't start until I return."

"That's wonderful. You'll do an amazing job."

Billy cleared his throat and asked, "Alice?"

"Yes?"

"The other day, I said something that maybe I shouldn't have said or was too forthright."

"And that was?"

"I was filled with so much emotion that I mentioned that I'd like to court you. I know you said that you'd like that, but I'm not sure if that was prudent—" he said but was interrupted.

"Prudent? What are you saying? I found it quite romantic, to be frank."

He shot her a shocked look and said, "You did?"

She took his hand and held it in between both of hers. "I did."

"I thought you might have thought it too forward."

"Not at all, but I do have a question. Why were you at the house? We had left each other at the end of the drive. All I knew was you were riding to town to inform them about the sheriff. I didn't know when or if I'd ever see you again, but there you were. I came out of that barn running for my very life, and when I set my eyes upon you, it was like looking at a guardian angel sent from God himself to save me. I knew then that I'd survive, that you'd finally put an end to the nightmare my family had been living."

"I came back to ask if I could court you," he confessed. "I couldn't just leave without you knowing how I felt about you. I care for you, Alice, and I think you're an amazing woman. I'd like to see you more. I want to spend time with you if you'd like to."

She squeezed his hand. Her eyes became wet with tears as she gave him a gentle smile. "I do want to spend time with you. The news that you're moving to Great Falls has filled my heart with a joy that I don't think I've ever felt. I know we only have known each other a short time, but there's something about you. I know that you didn't just show up at my door; we were meant to meet."

"I like to look at it that way too."

"Do you have to leave?"

"I do. I need to do one more thing, and then I can put this all behind me," Billy said.

"Please tell me you'll be safe and that you'll return."

"I will. I have no intention of getting hurt."

"When are you leaving?" she asked.

"Soon."

"So not right now. Good, let's chat some," she said happily.

The two spent ten minutes discussing anything but what had happened to them over the past week. It was a nice reprieve and gave them both a glimpse at what life would be like together. They laughed and teased and even began to talk about children of all things—not theirs but how they would be if they had children.

The door opened and in stepped Maggie. "It's time for you to go, Marshal. Alice needs to get her rest."

"Ma, you're looking at the new sheriff!" Alice chirped joyfully.

Maggie's face told Billy everything he needed to know. "You're the new sheriff?"

"Yes, ma'am. I'll start when I return from a short trip," Billy said.

"I can assume I'll be seeing more of you?" Maggie asked.

Billy gave Alice a warm smile and said, "That is correct, ma'am. I wish to court Alice…with your permission, of course."

With her arms folded, Maggie stood silent and motionless, her eyes fixed on Billy. "You'd like to court my Alice?"

"Yes, ma'am."

"Please, Ma, I'm eighteen and—"

"You may court my Alice, but only because I think you're an honorable man, and you did save us, so knowing you'll be around does make me feel…safer," Maggie said, her comment a departure from her normal curt replies. "But now you must go. Alice needs some rest." Maggie marched to the window and closed the curtains.

"I'll be back soon, I promise," he said to Alice. He got up, walked to the door, and turned towards her. "Until then, take care of yourself, Miss Alice."

"Bye," she said, giving him a wave.

Billy exited the room, closing the door behind him. Pure joy filled every ounce of his being. The only way he could describe the feeling was that he was in love with her. It seemed so odd to have such feelings for someone after only a short time, but he did. He enjoyed everything about her and would be counting the days until he saw her again. His mind then filled with what had to be done next, and that too gave him a bit of joy. He knew his days of being a marshal were close to being over, but until then he'd use the rights and privileges that came with the job to help him find the one last person he needed to find, and that was George Cummins.

EPILOGUE

JULY 30, 1895

VANCOUVER, BRITISH COLUMBIA, CANADA

G eorge Cummins belched loudly then exhaled his tainted breath inside the carriage.

His wife, Marie, shot him a disgusted look and brought her handkerchief to her face to cover her nose and mouth. "You're crude, George."

"If we're in the carriage much longer, it'll be coming out the other end." He chuckled.

"Vile, you're a vile man," she said. If one were to meet Marie, they'd marvel at her youthful beauty and delicate features. She was thirty years younger than George and married him primarily so she could live a privileged lifestyle. She had no love for the man minus his wealth and influence and could often be found in deep prayer, praying for the day he'd collapse from a heart attack or stroke.

George was sixty-five but looked every bit ten years older. His fat and bloated body always looked misshapen in the clothes he wore two sizes too small. Each step he'd take, his belly would jiggle and his chin would quiver. If he had to survive in the wilderness, he'd no doubt die within hours. He lacked any ability outside law and the ways of money but did find comfort in attending the occasional opera, which they were returning from.

He'd risen up the ranks of polite society and used the wealth he'd garnered through a trading company to secure his position on the prestigious Supreme Court in the province of British Columbia. There would exercise his power as a justice not only to expand the power of government but to his own financial gain if he could.

When he'd received news that his son, Al, was a wanted man, he sprang into action with hopes of saving Al from the hangman's noose. But truth be told, George wasn't concerned about his son's life; he'd forsaken him years before. No, it was to protect his own reputation. Using his vast influence, he'd contacted counterparts in the United States and worked that angle while he dispatched a team to go retrieve him. When the word reached him that Al had been arrested, all his years of influence proved fruitful, and he was able to ensure Al would be brought north and turned over to him. Yet he still had his team in the field. Never one to trust certain lawmen, George wanted to make sure his men reached Al first, and that was exactly what happened.

After the shoot-out outside Great Falls and Al's subsequent death, George breathed a sigh of relief; no longer would his son be a potential political burden for him. He knew that one man had survived the ordeal, and that man was Billy Connolly. Assured by the United States Attorney in Idaho that Billy was harmless, George withdrew his concern and went on with his life. He had swept it all under the rug and was now able to move on, or so he thought.

The carriage stopped outside the three-story walk-up row house. The red brick glistened from a rain shower that had spread across the city not an hour earlier.

"Ah, good, we're home," George said.

The driver jumped down and opened the carriage door. "Here you go, sir."

Marie exited the carriage first and rushed to the front door without saying a word to the driver.

George slid to the door and slipped out the door sideways; this was the only way he could get his girth out the door.

"Have a good evening, sir," the driver said.

George stood on the sidewalk and belched. He adjusted his trousers and said, "Good night, William."

"Same time in the morning, sir?" William asked.

"Not tomorrow, I'm sleeping in; then I have an interview with a man from the paper," George said.

"Right, sir, I'll see you the day after, then?" William asked.

"Correct, be here at seven on Thursday," George said. With his walking stick in his right hand, he sauntered to the front door, which stood open. He slowly ascended the brick stairs and entered the darkened foyer. "Marie, why didn't Anita light any lanterns?" Anita was the housemaid and had served George for a number of years.

Marie didn't reply.

"Marie, do you hear me!" George hollered up the

dark stairs that sat just a few feet in front of him.

Still no reply.

George set his walking stick down on a small table, removed his overcoat and hat, and hung them on a hook. "Marie?"

Silence.

"Damn woman, always ignoring me," George complained. He made it to the stairs, looked up and said, "Marie?"

No response came.

"Where is that damn fool woman?" he asked. He walked back to the table by aid of the light that came from the gas lamps outside on the street, found a lantern, and lit it. The orange flame came to life and lit the small space. "Sometimes you just have to do things yourself."

"That's right," Billy said, emerging from the shadows. He cocked his Colt and placed the muzzle against the back of George's head. "Sometimes you have to do things yourself."

George flinched, almost dropping the lantern. "Who are you? What do you want?"

"I came to talk," Billy said. "Now go into your parlor and have a seat."

"I have money. Is that what you want?" George said.

"Go into the parlor and I'll tell you what I want," Billy said.

George didn't hesitate. He briskly walked into the parlor; the light from the lantern showed him where Marie had been the entire time. "Why didn't you warn me?"

"On account that he had a gun to my head," Marie replied curtly.

"Take a seat," Billy ordered.

George sat next to Marie on a tufted loveseat near a large bay window. He placed the lantern on a coffee table and folded his hands in his lap.

Billy sat across from them in a similar loveseat, his pistol aimed at George.

"Who are you?" George asked.

"I'd tell you, but then I'd also have to kill her, and to be honest, I don't want to do that. She's been very nice and accommodating," Billy said, giving Marie a smile.

"Thank you," Marie replied.

"Don't be nice to him. He's a murderer or maybe a thief. Do you know who I am? Do you?" George spat.

"I do know; that's why I'm here," Billy said.

"You're making a mistake that will result in your swinging from a rope on the gallows," George threatened.

"I'm holding the gun and you're giving me threats, that is comical," Billy said.

"What do you want?" George asked.

"To be honest, what I want you can't give me," Billy said.

"And what is that?"

"The life of my friend," Billy answered.

"Who was your friend?"

"You sent men to rescue your son, Albert, which resulted in my good friend and partner getting murdered by your thugs," Billy replied, knowing his answer would tell George exactly who he was.

"You're that pesky US Marshal," George said.

"Now look what you've done. You put your wife's life in danger," Billy quipped. He had no intention of killing her, but he was having fun making idle threats.

"Don't kill me. I won't say a word. I didn't even know his son. You see, I married him after George divorced Al's mother."

"Marie, I'm not here to kill you, but I am here to kill your husband," Billy confessed.

"Kill me, for what? I didn't pull the trigger. I didn't do a damn thing," George roared.

Billy lifted the pistol, aimed it at George's face, and said, "You ordered them to kill us."

"I did not do such a thing," George bellowed.

"Are you really here to kill him?" Marie asked.

With a devilish smile, Billy replied, "I am, ma'am."

Marie cocked her head, gave George a vicious gaze, and said, "Kill him, please. He's the vilest human being I've ever met."

Dismayed by Marie's declaration, George asked, "You want me dead?"

"I do. I think you're disgusting," Marie spat.

"I'm disgusting? You prance around town shopping and acting like a harlot," George fired back.

Billy sat back, amused by the bickering.

"You call being nice to people equal to being a harlot, but you know something, George, if I did want to bed other men, who would blame me? Have you ever looked at yourself? You're a slug. I cringe every time you put your fat pudgy hands on me." She faced Billy and said, "I'll pay you to kill him."

"How dare you?" George declared.

"Ma'am, I don't need your money, but your discretion in this matter would be helpful even though I don't need it," Billy said, referring to an alibi he had already established for himself.

"I won't say a peep," she said.

"I will divorce you the very second this is over," George barked. "I'll then use every ounce of my power in the town to have you thrown out of every societal circle you're a part of."

"You think you're going to survive this night?" Billy asked George.

"Of course I am. You may have come here to kill me, but I have what every man and woman wants, and that's money," George said. "I'll give you whatever your heart desires if you'll just leave. What happened here won't ever be mentioned again. We will forget this night ever happened."

Billy pretended to ponder the idea, taking a long pause, then answered, "You think I'm a fool, don't you? The second I'd take your money, you'd release every lawman north and south of the border to go after me. No, I'm not here to take your money, I'm here to take your life."

"You don't want money?" George asked.

"Kill him," Marie spat.

"Shut up," George hollered at her. Facing Billy, he said, "I beg you, don't kill me. I didn't order them to hurt anyone. I merely wanted my son home safely."

"Mr. Cummins, I'm a man of the law, I believe in that more than anything, but some men, men like you, abuse it and try to live above it. Not this time. I'm here to correct that. I can't have you arrested. I couldn't even bring accusations about you that would see the light of day. No, if men like you are to receive the justice they deserve, it has to come from men like me willing to exercise violence in a righteous way."

"Please don't kill me, please," George pleaded, seeing that Billy seemed intent on killing him.

"Kill him. Release me from this prison," Marie urged.

"Ma'am, I am shocked by you," Billy said.

George scooted off the loveseat and plopped down on his knees. He clasped his hands together and said, "Please don't take my life. I'm really not a bad man."

"Yes, he is. He's one of the most corrupt people in this town," Marie said.

George smacked Marie with the back of his hand and barked, "Shut your mouth, woman!"

Marie's head snapped back.

"I said to shut up!" George yelled, his hand cocked back ready to strike again.

Marie brought her head forward; a dribble of blood came from the corner of her mouth.

Billy could see the anger welling up inside her. She jumped to her feet and took hold of Billy's pistol by the barrel and twisted it out of his hand. She placed it against George's temple and pulled the trigger.

The opposite side of George's head exploded. He

toppled to the floor dead.

Billy immediately took the pistol back. His mouth hung open. "You killed him."

"He hit me and you were only talking, so I did you a favor. Now you can go home knowing that you don't have blood on your hands," Marie said.

"But you just murdered your husband," Billy said in awe at the grisly event he'd just witnessed.

"What you saw tonight was just a glimpse into how my life with him has been. He regularly took to beating me. When I said he was a vile human being, I was telling you the truth," Marie said.

Billy didn't know what else to say. He'd come all that way to kill the one man who'd started this whole thing, only to have that opportunity taken from him by a wife who had been living in a nightmare situation.

"You'd best go now. A constable will no doubt arrive shortly, and if I'm going to play this up, I need to get ready," Marie said.

Billy holstered his pistol and said, "Goodbye."

"I trust you'll never utter a word of this?" she asked.

"You'll never see or hear from me ever again," Billy said. He turned and exited out the back where he'd entered. He raced down the alley and disappeared into the night.

AUGUST 9, 1895

TWO MILES SOUTH OF GREAT FALLS, MONTANA

Billy sat high in the saddle and gazed upon Alice's house in the distance. This was the very spot he'd left her weeks before, only to find her running for her life from Joseph. Now he had returned, his mission complete and a new badge on his chest. He was the sheriff of Cascade County and would now call Great Falls his new home. He didn't know what the future held, but what he did know was that Alice would be a part of any future he had.

He'd come a long way from his days living in Wallace, Idaho. He had always been an impulsive man who had to develop discipline to keep himself on the straight and narrow. It helped that he'd had Hemsworth as a friend and mentor, and even though he was gone, his lessons would stay with him his entire life.

The encounter with Al Cummins and Joseph had taught him that a good man is not necessarily a peaceful man, that sometimes evil men who use violence must be confronted by good men trained and willing to use violence. He'd also come to discover that the laws on the books weren't implemented equally and in a fair manner. He promised that as sheriff, he'd not just do what the laws said, but what was the right thing to do. Laws were written by men, and he'd come to find out that some men could bend those laws to their own benefit.

Filled with promise for what tomorrow and the days

after had in store, he headed down the drive and into a new life.

THE END

ABOUT THE AUTHOR

G. Michael Hopf is the best-selling and acclaimed author of THE NEW WORLD series and other novels. He spent two decades living a life of adventure before he settled down and became a novelist full time. He is a combat veteran of the United States Marine Corps and a former executive protection agent. He lives with his family in San Diego, CA

Please feel free to contact him at geoff@gmichaelhopf.com with any questions or comments.

www.gmichaelhopf.com

www.facebook.com/gmichaelhopf

BOOKS by G. MICHAEL HOPF

THE NEW WORLD SERIES

THE END
THE LONG ROAD
SANCTUARY
THE LINE OF DEPARTURE
BLOOD, SWEAT & TEARS
THE RAZOR'S EDGE
THOSE WHO REMAIN

THE NEW WORLD SERIES SPIN OFFS

NEMESIS: INCEPTION
EXIT

THE WANDERER SERIES

VENGEANCE ROAD
BLOOD GOLD
TORN ALLEGIANCE

THE BOUNTY HUNTER SERIES

LAST RIDE
THE LOST ONES
PRAIRIE JUSTICE

ADDITIONAL APOCALYPTIC BOOKS

HOPE (CO-AUTHORED W/ A. AMERICAN)
DAY OF RECKONING
DETOUR: AN APOCALYPTIC HORROR STORY
DRIVER 8: A POST-APOCALYPTIC NOVEL
THE DEATH TRILOGY (CO-AUTHORED WITH JOHN
W. VANCE)

ADDITIONAL WESTERN BOOKS

THE LAWMAN
THE RETRIBUTION OF LEVI BASS
JUDGMENT DAY

68199000R00138

Made in the USA
Columbia, SC
05 August 2019